STO

ACPL ITEM
DISCA P9-EDO-442

MEMOIRS
OF A FUGITIVE

Adapted by Barbara Ritchie:

LIFE AND TIMES OF FREDERICK DOUGLASS

MEMOIRS OF A FUGITIVE:
America's First Antislavery Novel

THE MIND AND HEART OF
FREDERICK DOUGLASS:
Excerpts from Speeches of the Great Negro Orator

MEMOIRS OF A FUGITIVE

America's First Antislavery Novel

by RICHARD HILDRETH
adapted by Barbara Ritchie

Thomas Y. Crowell Company   *New York*

Acknowledgments

In the short biography of Richard Hildreth on page 196 the facts of Hildreth's life and critical appraisals of his life and work have been taken from Donald E. Emerson's study, "Richard Hildreth", published in *The Johns Hopkins University Studies in Historical and Political Science*, v. 64, pp. 337–513. Had Dr. Emerson not chosen Richard Hildreth as the subject of his doctoral thesis in 1946, we would be dependent on the dry facts of the encyclopedists for answers to the question, "Who was Richard Hildreth?" We acknowledge with gratitude our debt to Dr. Emerson's valuable work.

COPYRIGHT © 1971 BY BARBARA RITCHIE
All rights reserved. Except for use in a review, the reproduction or utilization of this work in any form or by any electronic, mechanical, or other means, now known or hereafter invented, including xerography, photocopying, and recording, and in any information storage and retrieval system is forbidden without the written permission of the publisher. Published simultaneously in Canada by Fitzhenry & Whiteside Limited, Toronto.

Manufactured in the United States of America

L.C. Card 74–146047
ISBN 0–690–52949–x

1   2   3   4   5   6   7   8   9   10

1614887

Introduction

The distinction of having written the first antislavery novel does not belong, as most of us would assume, to Harriet Beecher Stowe for her celebrated *Uncle Tom's Cabin, or Life Among the Lowly,* but to Richard Hildreth for his forgotten *The Slave; or Memoirs of Archy Moore.* Richard Hildreth's novel was published in 1836, Harriet Beecher Stowe's not until 1852.

To Richard Hildreth belongs another, and perhaps fatal, "first." As the critic Lorenzo Dow Turner has pointed out, Hildreth was the first American writer to portray any but cowed and passive slaves. But Hildreth went even further. Implicit in his novel is the statement that slaves were endowed with the spirit and all the proud attributes of full manhood which whites arrogated to themselves alone. Hildreth's assertion, if accepted, would have demolished a cherished racial myth. The myth was protected, though, and *The Slave* consigned to oblivion by the simple expedient of the refusal of critics or the reading public, for well over a century, to acknowledge its existence in literature or in history.

Sixteen years after they had spurned *The Slave,* Americans seized the opportunity to eulogize the black man of their fantasy—the ineffectual, harmless, humble, lachrymose, and saintly Uncle Tom—by making *Uncle Tom's Cabin* the first American best seller to sell a million copies in the United States alone. In dramatized form it played continuously throughout the nation from 1853 until 1930, and for seventy-seven long years of performances in the small towns of America "there wasn't a dry eye in the house." Only with the advent of the Great Depression did the playbills come down; people could no longer afford the luxury of tears for the "lowly." All that is left of Uncle Tom is an entry in the dictionary. He has taken his place in the language as a derogatory epithet, meaning "a Negro who is held to be humiliatingly subservient or deferential to whites." "Uncle Tom" is used by blacks and whites alike as a term of abuse and contempt.

Hildreth and Stowe were contemporaries, although he was five years her senior. Both were opposed to slavery, but Hildreth was from the beginning what Stowe never became: an abolitionist. Hildreth was not only *against* slavery, on moral and ethical grounds, but passionately *for* doing away with the "peculiar institution" as soon as possible, through an unrelenting attack on the customs, laws, and institutions that fortressed it. To the vast majority of Americans of his day, Hildreth and his ilk were at the least wildly radical, if not diabolical. Stowe, an evangelist, proclaimed slavery to be a sin of which we were all guilty. Hildreth, a humanist, pronounced it a social crime for which we were all equally responsible. We chose to agonize over our guilt rather than to face the arduous task of setting right an unconscionable wrong.

vi

Before beginning her novel, Stowe informed her editor that she would "show the *best* side of the thing and something *faintly approaching* the *worst*." After careful scrutiny, Hildreth was unable to detect a "best side" of an evil thing. "The whole system is totally and radically wrong."

It was Hildreth's novel that was dropped from history and from literature. In five generations of compulsory free education we have not been compelled to learn anything about a novel written by a young man of intellectual honesty, creative imagination, and a realistic way of reporting the human truth of the human tragedy of slavery.

Barbara Ritchie

Contents

All men are by nature equally free and independent, and have certain *inherent rights,* of which, when they enter into society, they cannot by any compact deprive or divest their posterity, viz: the enjoyment of life and liberty, with the means of acquiring and possessing property, and pursuing happiness and safety.   —Virginia Bill of Rights, Article I

Prologue

You who would know what evils man can inflict upon his fellow without reluctance or regret, who would learn the limit of human endurance—and with what bitter anguish the heart may swell and yet not burst—peruse these memoirs!

My story may perhaps touch even some of those who are themselves the authors of misery similar to that which I endured. Should I accomplish no more than this, that the story of my wrongs summon up in the mind of a single oppressor the dark images of his own misdeeds and teach his conscience how to torture him with the picture of himself, I shall be content. For next to the tears and the exultations of the emancipated, the remorse of tyrants is the choicest offering upon the altar of liberty.

But perhaps something more may be possible—not likely, but to be imagined and even faintly hoped for. Perhaps within some youthful breast I may be able to rekindle the embers of humanity. Perhaps in spite of habits and prejudices that have been fostered from earliest childhood; perhaps in spite of the allurements of wealth and political distinction and the still stronger allurements of indolence and ease; in spite of the pratings of priests and the arguments of time-serving sophists; in spite of the terrors of the weak-spirited and wavering; in spite of evil precept and evil example, perhaps he may dare—that generous and heroic youth!—to cherish and avow the feelings of a man.

My appeal is to that youth who in the midst of tyrants dares to preach the good tidings of liberty. In the very school of oppression, he stands boldly forth, the advocate of human rights. He breaks down the ramparts of prejudice. He dissipates the illusions of avarice and pride. He repeals the sacrilegious enactments which, though destitute of every feature of justice, have usurped the sacred form of law. He snatches the whip from the hand of the master and breaks forever the fetter of the slave!

Instrument of mercy and illustrious deliverer, come quickly!—for if your coming be delayed, there may come in your place one who will be not only *deliverer* but *avenger*.

Chapter 1

The country in which I was born was then one of the richest and most populous in eastern Virginia. My father, Colonel Charles Moore, was the head of one of the influential families in that part of the country; and family, at the time I was born, was a thing of no slight consequence in lower Virginia.

Nature and education had conspired to qualify Colonel Moore to fill with credit the station in which his birth had placed him. He was a finished aristocrat, and there was in his bearing a conscious superiority which few could resist. He was spoken of among his friends and neighbors as the faultless pattern of a true *Virginia* gentleman, by which they supposed themselves to convey the highest possible praise.

When the American Revolution broke out in 1775, Colonel Moore was but a lad of ten or twelve years, and thus his adolescence and young manhood coincided with the most fateful and stirring decade in the history of America. By birth and education he belonged to the aristocratic party and was, of course, conservative. But

1

the impulses of youth and patriotism were too strong to be resisted. He espoused with zeal the cause of liberty, did what he could to promote it, and was always its warm and energetic admirer. Among my earliest recollections of him is the earnestness with which, among his friends and guests, he used to vindicate the cause of the French Revolution, which began only five years after we won our freedom, and which lasted as long as our own. Although I understood little or nothing of what he said, the spirit and eloquence with which he spoke could not fail to affect me. The *rights of man* and the *rights of human nature* were phrases which I heard so often repeated that they made an indelible impression upon me.

But Colonel Moore was not a mere talker. He was credited with acting up to his principles and was universally regarded as a man of the greatest good nature, honor, and uprightness. The tenderness of his heart, his benevolence, and his sympathy with misfortune were traits of his character which were spoken of by everybody.

Had I been allowed to choose my own paternity, could I possibly have selected a more desirable father? But, by the laws and customs of Virginia, it is not the father but the mother whose rank and condition determine that of the child. My mother was a concubine and a slave.

Yet those who beheld her for the first time would hardly have imagined that she was connected with a race considered so ignoble and degraded. She could boast the most brilliant black-eyed beauty. One could seek in vain to find her rival among the pale and languid ladies of eastern Virginia! Her black heritage, however remote, was known; and because of it alone, she was consigned to the most degraded situation possible for her, especially among "respectable" white ladies. In her own eyes, of course, my poor mother had risen to the highest station possible for a slave woman in Virginia, and took no little satisfaction in her accomplishment. At any rate, her beauty was notorious through that part of the country. Colonel Moore could pride himself upon owning the swiftest horse and the handsomest wench in all Virginia.

The Colonel was married to a woman who was amiable enough and whom, I dare say, he loved and respected. In the course of time she bore him two daughters and two sons. This circumstance did not hinder him, any more than it does any other American planter, from giving a very free indulgence to his amorous temperament among his numerous slaves at Spring Meadow, for so his estate was called. Many of the young women had occasion to boast of his attentions.

My mother was for several years distinguished by Colonel Moore's very particular regard. She brought him four children, all of whom except myself, the eldest, were lucky enough to have died in infancy. In appearance I favored my father's coloring and could easily have been mistaken for a white child; but from my mother I inherited some imperceptible portion of African blood, and with it the base and cursed condition of a slave. But though born a slave, as regards natural endowments, whether of mind or body, I am bold to assert that my father had more reason to be proud of me than of either of his legitimate and acknowledged sons.

3

A maxim well understood, in that part of the world in which it was my misfortune to be born, is this: *That education which commences earliest is the most effective.* And as it sometimes happens in eastern Virginia that half a man's children are born masters and the other half are born slaves, it has become sufficiently obvious how necessary it is to begin early the course of discipline proper to train them up for these very different situations. It is the general custom that "Young Master" almost from the hour of his birth has allotted to him some little slave near his own age upon whom he begins, from the time that he can walk alone, to practice his apprenticeship of tyranny. Within less than a year after my birth, Colonel Moore's wife presented him with her second son, James, and I was duly appointed to be the body servant of my younger brother. It is in my capacity as Master James's boy that, following back the traces of memory, I first discover myself.

The usual consequences of giving one child absolute authority over another may be easily imagined. The love of domination is perhaps the strongest of our passions, and it is surprising how soon the veriest child will become perfect in the practice of tyranny.

Of this, Colonel Moore's eldest son, Master William, was a striking instance. He was the terror not only of Joe, his own boy, but of all the children on the place. That unthinking and irrational delight in the exercise of cruelty which is sometimes displayed by a wayward child seemed in him almost a passion that soon developed into a habit. He always went armed with a whip twice as long as himself, and upon the least opposition to his whims Master William was ready to

4

show his skill in the use of it. He took some pains to conceal all this from his father. Colonel Moore himself, however, was pretty careful not to see what he could by no means approve of but what at the same time (indulgent father that he was!) he would have found it very difficult to prevent or to cure.

My master, James, was a very different boy. Sickly and weak from his birth, his temper was gentle and his mind effeminate. He had an affectionate disposition and soon conceived a fondness for me which I unhesitatingly returned. He protected me from Master William's tyrannies by his entreaties, his tears, and—what had much more weight—his threats of complaining to his father.

I was easily able to pardon and to put up with occasional pettishness and ill humor from Master James. His bad health furnished ample excuse for it. By flattery and apparent servility (for a child learns and practices such arts as readily as a man), I presently came to have great influence over him. He was the master and I the slave, but since we were both children this artificial distinction had less potency. I found little difficulty in maintaining that actual superiority to which my superior vigor, both of body and mind, so justly entitled me.

Master James's formal education was begun when he reached the age of five years. To learn the letters was a laborious undertaking for which my young master seemed to have no genius whatever. He indeed wanted to learn. It was the ability, not the inclination, that was lacking. By putting our heads together, we soon hit upon a plan. We arranged that the family tutor would first teach me the letters, which I was gradually, as opportunity served, to instill into the mind of Master James. This plan we found to answer admirably. Neither the tutor nor Colonel Moore made any objection to it. All that Colonel Moore desired was that his son should learn to read and write, and the tutor was very willing to shift the most laborious part of his task to my shoulders.

As yet no one had dreamed of those barbarous and abominable laws—unparalleled in any other codes, and destined to be the everlasting disgrace of America—those laws by which it has now been made a crime, punishable with fine and imprisonment, to teach a slave to read! At the present time, not custom alone but the laws, too, have openly become a party to this accursed conspiracy! Yes, I believe the tyrants would tear out our very eyes (and that by virtue of a regularly enacted statute!) had they ingenuity enough to invent a way of enabling us to delve and drudge without them.

I soon learned to read and before long made Master James almost as good a reader as myself. As my young master's studies progressed, the plan of first teaching me and then him was abandoned. Yet I had a desire to learn and found no difficulty, while in attendance on him in the schoolroom, in extracting the substance of the lessons. In this way I acquired some knowledge of arithmetic and geography and even a smattering of Latin.

I took great pains to conceal what knowledge I had acquired; for while it increased my standing among the servants, it also exposed me to a good deal of ridicule among the whites, to which ridicule I was very sensitive.

6

I was not looked upon in 1816 (as I would be today, twenty years later) as a dreadful monster, breathing war and rebellion and plotting to cut the throats of all white people in America! I was, instead, regarded as a sort of a freak, a three-legged hen or a sheep with four eyes, a thing to be produced and exhibited for the entertainment of strangers. Frequently at a dinner party, after the wine had circulated pretty freely, I was set to read paragraphs in the newspapers to amuse my master's tipsy guests. I was then puzzled, perplexed, and tormented by all sorts of absurd and impertinent questions, which I was obliged to answer under penalty of having a wine glass, a bottle, or a plate flung at my head. Master William, especially, made me the butt of his wit. He took great pride in calling me "the learned nigger," a name he had invented for me, though God knows that my cheek was little less fair than his own.

It may be thought that these were trifling vexations. In truth, they were. Yet it cost me many a struggle before I could learn to endure them with any tolerable patience. I was compensated in some measure by the pleasure I took in listening, as I stood behind my master's chair, to the conversation of the company.

Colonel Moore kept open house and almost every day had guests at his table. He was himself an eloquent and most agreeable talker, and always expressed himself with a great deal of point and vivacity. Many of his friends were men who were well informed in politics and a great variety of other subjects, and they also entertained his liberal opinions on political matters. When I heard them talk of equal rights and declaim against tyranny and oppression, my heart swelled with emotions of which I scarcely understood the meaning.

All this time I made no personal application of what I heard and felt. I became enamored only of the abstract beauty of liberty and equality. It was the French republicans with whom I sympathized, it was the Austrian and English tyrants against whom my indignation was aroused. I had not yet learned to think about myself. What I saw around me, I had always been accustomed to see, and all appeared to me to be the fixed order of nature.

I was singularly fortunate in my young master, to whom I was as much a companion as a servant. By his favor, and because my mother continued a favorite with Colonel Moore, I enjoyed more indulgences than any other servant on the place. Comparing my situation with that of a field hand, I might pronounce myself fortunate indeed. Although I was exposed to mortifications enough to give me a foretaste of the bitter cup which everyone who lives a slave must swallow, my youth and the buoyant vivacity of my temper as yet sustained me. And I was sustained, too, by the wonderful freedom we experienced when Master James enjoyed one of his spells of good health and keen spirits, and wheedled for us from the stables two old reliable horses, and we were allowed to set forth to explore the neighborhood. We got more speed out of the nags than our elders would have thought possible and roamed farther afield than they dreamed.

At this time I did not know that Colonel Moore was my father. That gentleman was indebted for no inconsiderable portion of his high reputation to a very strict attention to those conventional observances which so

8

often usurp the place of morals. It is considered no crime whatever for a master to be, if he chooses, the father of every infant slave born upon his plantation. Yet it is esteemed, especially in Virginia and generally throughout the South, a very grave breach of propriety for such a father ever to acknowledge or take notice of any of his unfortunate slave children. Colonel Moore had the Virginia gentleman's indescribable horror at the thought of violating any of the settled proprieties of the society in which he moved. Although a republican in politics, he certainly was very much an aristocrat and an exclusive in his feelings.

The secret which my father did not choose, and my mother did not dare, to communicate to me, I might perhaps have obtained from my fellow servants, had I enjoyed their trust and friendship. But, as did most of the lighter-skinned slaves, I felt contempt for my duskier brothers in misfortune. I kept myself as much as possible at a distance from them. I scorned to associate with men a little darker than myself. So ready are slaves to imbibe the ridiculous prejudices of their oppressors, and thus themselves add new links to the chains which deprive them of their liberty!

But let me do my father justice. Though he never made the slightest acknowledgement of our relationship, there was a tone of good-natured indulgence whenever he spoke to me. His natural kindliness seemed, when directed toward me, to have something special in it. He succeeded in captivating my affections, and I loved him sincerely.

Chapter 2

I was about seventeen years old when my mother was attacked by an illness which proved fatal to her. She had a presentiment of her fate and sent for me. After the woman who nursed her left us, she asked me to sit down beside her bed. I tried to conceal my alarm at finding her so pale and weak.

She began by saying, in a voice that lacked all force of expression, that she feared she would die and she wanted me to know something of her life. Her mother, she said, had been a slave; her father, a certain Colonel Randolph, scion of one of the great Virginia families. She had been raised as a lady's maid. When Colonel Moore married, he purchased her and presented her to his wife. She was then but a girl; but as she grew older and her beauty became more noticeable, she found much favor in the eyes of her master. She was given a neat little house and lived, from then on, a very careless, indolent, but, as she told me, a very unhappy life.

I must here digress to say that for much of this unhappiness she was indebted to herself. The airs of superiority she assumed in her intercourse with the other slaves induced them to improve every opportunity of vexing and mortifying her. This foolish pride arose in her, as a similar feeling did in me, because our situation was so superior to that of most of the other slaves that we naturally imagined ourselves to belong to a superior race.

It was doubtless under the influence of this feeling that my mother, having told me who my father was, was able to smile, ill as she was, and to say that I had running in my veins the best blood of Virginia—the blood of the Moores and the Randolphs! Alas, she did not seem to recollect that though I might count all the nobility of Virginia among my ancestors, one drop of blood imported from Africa (though that, too, might be the blood of kings and chieftains!) would condemn me to perpetual slavery.

The secret she revealed of my birth made, at that time, little impression on me. My anxiety was for her and for the terrible possibility of her death and of losing a tender and affectionate parent. It was after her death and after the sharpness of my grief had abated somewhat, that my thoughts began to dwell on what she had told me. I hardly know how to describe the effect which it seemed to have upon me. Nor is it easy to tell what was its actual effect, or what ought to be ascribed to other and more general causes. Perhaps that revolution of feeling which I now experienced should be attributed in a great measure to the change from boyhood to manhood through which I was passing.

My mind seemed to be filled with indefinite anxieties. There was an unsatisfied craving for something, I knew not what, a longing which I could do nothing to satisfy because I could not tell its object. I would often be lost in thought, but my mind did not seem to fix itself on any certain aim; and after an hour of apparently the deepest meditation, I should have been very much at a loss to tell what it was I had been thinking about.

Sometimes my reflections would take a more definite shape. I would begin to consider what I was and what I had to anticipate. I was the son of a free man, yet born to be a slave. I had been endowed by nature with abilities which I should never be permitted to exercise. I was possessed of knowledge which already I found it expedient to conceal. The slave of my own father, the servant of my own brother, I was a bounded, limited, confined, and captive creature who did not dare to go out of sight of his master's house without a written permission to do so! The awful certainty possessed me that I was destined to be the sport of I knew not whose caprices, to be forbidden in anything to act for myself or to consult my own happiness, destined to labor all my life at another's bidding and liable every hour and instant of my life to suffer most outrageous oppressions and degrading humiliations. I struggled hard to suppress these bitter reflections, but again and again the hateful ideas would start up and sting me into anguish.

My young master continued to be as kind as ever, and indeed there was a strong bond of friendship between us. Yet I was changing into a man (although still called "boy") while he, alas, seemed yet a boy. His protracted ill health had checked his physical growth and appeared also to have affected his mental maturity. At

12

the same time, what I can only describe as the gentleness and sweetness of his nature was in no way impaired.

He would sometimes find me in tears, and sometimes when I was lost in thought, he would complain of my inattention. I had no difficulty in putting him off with plausible excuses, for deceit and the art of disguising one's true feelings are lifesaving devices a slave learns almost as early as he learns to walk. As often as Master James would say, "Come, Archy boy, let me know what it is that troubles you," I would as often make light of the matter, and soon we would be laughing together. Every day my attachment for him grew stronger, as indeed it might, for he was my sole hope. As long as I remained with him, I could expect to escape the utter bitterness of slavery.

I took now to reading to my young master from the Bible, not for the religious messages but for the stories to be found there. I had long outgrown the earlier, childish books that we had read so often—and he cared not at all what I read, so long as my voice was heard relating a story.

I turned again and again to the story of Hagar, the bondwoman, and Ishmael, her son. As I read how an angel came to their relief when the hard-hearted Abraham had driven them into the wilderness, there sprang up within me a wild, uncertain hope that through some accident, I knew not what, I too might find succor and relief. This irrational hope would be followed by new bitterness, and I felt, with awful certainty, that I was another Ishmael wandering in the wilderness, every

13

man's hand against me and my hand against every man. That James never made the connection in his mind that I made in mine, seeing myself as Ishmael, goes without saying. I was his slave, but he did not know me as that; his feeling toward me was that I was a good and equal companion.

In the Colonel's house and among the slaves as well, all at Spring Meadow had known that Master James could never live to full maturity; yet I was not prepared for his final decline and fatal illness. I did not so much pray for his recovery as I willed it, with tireless and tender attentions. Never was a master more faithfully served; but it was the friend and companion, not the slave, who served Master James.

There was little praying done over the dying boy. Ours was a liberal and free-thinking household. Colonel Moore had no time for the kind of exhorting, evangelical religion that the slaves and the more common among the whites subscribed to—the only kind of religion available in the region. When the fatal crisis came, Master James's weeping family and friends collected about his bed. He struggled for breath and gasped out in a whisper, "Archy, help me." I lifted him up, so that he might breathe more easily. He died in my arms.

The family of Colonel Moore well knew how truly I had loved my young master. They respected the profound depth of my grief for a month or more and asked nothing of me. I mourned Master James. But as the temperament of the mind is ever changing, I no longer felt the degree of anxious apprehension for myself that I had known earlier when I had contemplated the loss of my only friend. Although his death was certain to

14

mean a radical change for me, I awaited my fate with a sort of stupid and careless indifference.

Although I might have been temporarily excused from waiting upon my master's table, I continued to do so as usual. Nobody called upon me to do anything or seemed to notice that I was present. Even Master William made an effort to repress his habitual insolence.

But this could not last. One morning after breakfast, Master William suddenly told his father that, in his opinion, the slaves at Spring Meadow were a great deal too indulgently treated. He was by this time a smart, dashing, elegant young man, having returned a year before from college and lately from a winter in Charleston, whither he had been sent, as his father expressed it, to wear off the rusticity of the schoolroom. It was there, perhaps, that he had learned the new precepts of humanity which he was now preaching.

He declared that any tenderness towards a slave only served to make him insolent and discontented and was quite thrown away on the ungrateful rascal. Then, looking about and his eye lighting upon me as if by innocent accident, he exclaimed, "There's that boy Archy, now. I'll bet a hundred to one that I could make him one of the best servants in the world. Nothing has spoiled him but poor James's overindulgence. Come, Father, just be good enough to give him to me, for I want another servant most devilishly."

Without stopping for an answer, he hastened out of the room, saying in parting that he had a cockfight to attend.

There was nobody else at the table. Colonel Moore turned towards me. He commended my faithful attachment to his poor James and said, "I hope that now you will transfer the same zeal and affection to Master William."

These words roused me in a moment. Gone was my lack of interest in what life might have in store for me. In horror and alarm I threw myself at my master's feet and begged him not to give me to Master William. The terms in which I spoke of his son, the terror I expressed at the thought of becoming his servant, made Colonel Moore as angry as I had ever seen him. The blood rushed to his face; his brow grew dark and contracted.

Seeing this, I despaired of escaping my wretched fate, and my despair drove me to a torrent of rash words. I begged him to consider my pleas as if they came from a son who loved him, as if it were his beloved James who pleaded. I dared—brokenly and inarticulately, because of the emotion that choked my throat—I dared to make an appeal to Colonel Moore's paternal feelings, but without, however, actually calling him "Father" or claiming to be his son.

As soon as I got the words out and saw the shock that caused the angry red to drain from my master's face, I hid my own face in my hands and was, in turn, shocked into the realization that I had just pronounced my own death sentence. I had committed the slave's unpardonable offense—impertinence. I would be turned over to Master William to die under his cruelty, or I would be sold to the Deep South to perish in the cruel rice swamps.

I would have retracted my words, but since that was impossible, I accepted my fate. I became almost calm. Colonel Moore was speaking, but it was some time before I could take in what he said to me. I was foolish, he said. I would one day regret refusing Master William's service. I was advised to change my mind. He could not understand my reluctance. However, if I persisted he was prepared to offer me a second choice. I could become a field hand.

I got to my feet, feeling almost too weak to stand. I thanked him profusely. I assured him that I would make one of the best field hands on the plantation. He glared at me and seemed genuinely disbelieving. We both knew the hard labor, scanty fare, and harsh treatment accorded field hands. Did I *prefer* the fields to the work of a manservant? he asked. My assurance that such was the case, and my repeated giving of thanks, at length convinced him. With a smile that was more of a sneer than a smile, he ordered me to report to Mr. Stubbs and dismissed me from his presence.

I have often thought since that what saved me on this occasion was a wisdom that I was not aware I possessed. I knew Colonel Moore in the way that oppressed people everywhere know their oppressors, by virtue of a constant, tense awareness and keen observation; for there is no attention so sharp and so concentrated as that given by a slave to a member of that class which, every instant, can pronounce his death sentence. Not in my mind, but perhaps in the depths of my soul, I knew that Colonel Moore could not hear what the "proprieties" demanded that he not hear. I had hinted at something that was not, because in polite, sober society it was not acknowledged to exist. Therefore my appeal had not been that of a son to his father. It had not even been an appeal from one human being to the humanity and conscience of another. It had not been an appeal at all. I had merely babbled. In Colonel Moore's mind, a slave had expressed a preference for field work, and kind and indulgent master that he was, he had granted the foolish wish.

Yet at other times I allowed myself to believe that Colonel Moore had a conscience and that I had touched it, that he had a paternal feeling for me and had been swayed by it. So great is the need for a son to believe he is loved by his father!

In all parts of slaveholding America with which I have become acquainted, an overseer is regarded with contempt not only by the slaves but by the slaveowners themselves. The young lady who dines heartily on lamb has a sentimental horror of the butcher who killed it. The slaveowner who lives luxuriously on the forced labor of his slaves has a like sentimental abhorrence of the man who holds the whip and compels the labor.

Our overseer, Mr. Stubbs, well deserved the contempt felt for him by all at Spring Meadow. He was a thickset, clumsy man of about fifty, with a little bullet head covered with short tangled hair and stuck close upon his shoulders. His face was curiously mottled and spotted. His talk in the field was a string of oaths from the midst of which it was not very easy to disentangle his meaning. "You damned black rascal" was pretty sure to begin every sentence, and "by God" to end it. And in his management of the plantation he used the whip as freely as his tongue.

Now Colonel Moore, having received a European education, had a great dislike of all *unnecessary* cruelty. About once a week he was made very angry by some

18

brutal act on the part of his overseer. He satisfied his outraged feelings by declaring himself very much offended, and thereupon suffered things to go on just as before. The truth was that Mr. Stubbs understood growing of crops. Such a man was too valuable to be given up.

Mr. Stubbs listened to my account of myself, all the time rolling his tobacco from one cheek to the other and squinting at me with his little, twinkling, gray eyes. Having cursed me to his satisfaction for "a damned fool," he ordered me to follow him to the field. A large clumsy hoe with a handle six feet long was put into my hands, and I was kept hard at work all day.

When I quit the field at dark, the overseer pointed out to me a miserable little hovel, about ten feet square and half as many high, without floor or window. This I was to share with Billy, a young slave of about my own age. I got permission to return to the big house to fetch my chest from the loft, and in this I carried away my few possessions.

By way of bed and bedding, I received a single blanket. A basket of corn and a pound of rancid bacon were given me as my week's allowance of provisions. Billy helped me beat my corn into meal and loaned me his kettle to cook it in, so that about midnight I was able to break a fast of some sixteen or twenty hours. The chest, sturdily made of stout planks by carpenters on the place, and intended originally to hold a greater cargo than my few possessions, served well enough as a bed. So great was my exhaustion, I could have slept on a bed of nails. Billy had filched, or been given, an old and badly torn horse blanket, and wrapped in this,

19

he lay down on the floor. Our accommodations were as good as we had any right to expect. And the labor in the field I considered better than the servitude I had escaped.

Allow me to move ahead of my story and to dispose of Master William, who appears no more in these memoirs. Within one year, his father had occasion to mourn the death of his remaining legitimate son. Master William had the misfortune to engage in a duel with a gentleman with whom he had had an argument at a cockfight, and one who could shoot more quickly and more accurately than could Master William. Colonel Moore was inconsolable for many months. I do not recall that this information, when I heard it spoken about among the slaves, was of much interest to me or that I felt any pity for the master.

Chapter 3

For the first few weeks of my life as a field hand, I followed my set purpose of being the most slavish of the toilers in the field. In spite of my almost constant hunger and the torture of forcing my body to such long hours of unaccustomed labor, I performed the same tasks as those who had been field hands all their lives. Even Mr. Stubbs had no fault to find but pronounced me, more than once, a "right likely hand."

The time came when he was no longer able to do so. Our cabin had a very leaky roof, and during rainy weather Billy and I found it slightly dank and disagreeable. We determined to repair it, and, to get time to do so by daylight, exerted ourselves to finish our tasks at an early hour. Billy, a dull fellow at best, followed my lead and raised no objection to the plan. Perhaps because I had lived almost all my life in the master's house, perhaps because I was white and Billy was accustomed to taking directions from that color, he made no objections to our walking out of the field when the time came. As for me, when with Master James, it was I who had made plans for our employment and had taken the lead in executing the plans. It is probable that we might have got permission to leave the field for our good purpose; but perhaps I was too young, even too arrogant, to imagine it necessary to petition for the favor of repairing one of the master's roofs!

It was about four o'clock in the afternoon, then, that we were returning to the long line of slave huts we called "the town" when Mr. Stubbs overtook us and asked why we had left the field. I told him that we had finished the work we had been set to do, whereupon he interrupted with his usual oaths and said that since we didn't have half enough to do, we could finish out the day by weeding his garden.

Billy turned in silence to do his bidding. But I ventured to say, as one reasonable man might say to another, that since we had finished our tasks it seemed very hard to give us additional work.

This put Mr. Stubbs into a perfect passion of fury. He swore twenty oaths and between oaths managed to convey that I should both weed the garden and be whipped into the bargain. He sprang from his horse, and catching me by the collar of my shirt (in the heat of the summer, slaves wore only this single garment), he lay upon me with his whip. The pain was great enough. The *idea* of being whipped was sufficiently bitter. But this degradation—that I had devoted every waking hour of the past weeks in avoiding—was in the end not so hard to bear as my sense of the *injustice* that was done me. It was with the utmost difficulty that I restrained myself from turning on my tormentor and dashing him to the ground. I took the lashing without outcry, bore the injury the best I could, and was then turned into the garden. The clouds breaking and the moon happening to be full, Billy and I were kept weeding until midnight.

My pain-racked body and my tortured mind allowed me to doze but fitfully during the short hours left of the dark. The next day was Sunday. I resolved to avail myself of the Sunday's leisure to complain to my master of the barbarous treatment I had experienced at the hands of Mr. Stubbs.

That slaves are allowed to put down their hoes on Sundays is the sole and single boon for which American slaves are indebted to the Christian religion. Slave-owners trample underfoot every other precept of the Gospel without the slightest hesitation, but so long as they do not compel their slaves to work on Sundays they think themselves well entitled to the name of Christians. Perhaps they are, but if so, a title so easily purchased can be worth but little.

Colonel Moore received me with coolness. However, he heard my story to the end. He even condescended to declare that nothing gave him so much pain as to have his servants unnecessarily or unreasonably punished. He told me to go about my business, having first assured me that he would see Mr. Stubbs and inquire into the matter. That was the last I heard from Colonel Moore.

That same evening Mr. Stubbs sent for me to come to his house. With the help of his assistant, who leaped upon me, he tied me to a tree before his door, gave me a goodly number of stripes across my still raw back, and advised me to go to the house again and complain if I dared.

"It's a damned hard case," he added, "if I can't lick a damned nigger's insolence out of him without being obliged to give an account of it!"

My mental anguish that night was extreme. I dwelt upon the treatment I had received that day until I was surely on the verge of madness. A blow is esteemed among free men as the very worst of indignities; and low as their oppressors may have sunk them, it is also esteemed an indignity among slaves.

Toward morning I began to understand a little the lesson I had learned that day, a lesson every slave must learn if he hopes to live. The slave learns that the only way to escape a repetition of injustice is to submit in silence to the first infraction, and to avoid where possible a repetition of the attitude or action that brought on the unjust reprisal. I digested the bitter lesson and acquired a portion of that hypocritical humility so necessary for slaves.

Humility! A slave must give at least the *appearance* of humility—for the master cares little whether it be real or pretended. In the master's eyes humility is the great and crowning virtue of the slave, who must exhibit a disposition to submit without complaint to every possible wrong and indignity, reply to the most unjust accusations with a soft voice and smiling face, take kicks, cuffs, and blows as though they were a favor, kiss the foot that grinds him into the dust!

This sort of humility was a virtue with which nature had but scantily endowed me. I found it desperately

24

hard to strip myself of all the feelings of a man. It was like quitting the erect carriage which I had received from God's hand and learning to crawl on the earth like a base reptile. This was indeed a hard lesson, but I learned it. An American overseer is a stern teacher, and if I learned but slowly, it was not the fault of Mr. Stubbs.

It would be irksome to myself and tedious to the reader to enter into a minute detail of all the miserable and monotonous incidents that made up my life at this time. A single sentence summing up this part of my history might suffice to describe *the whole lifetimes of many thousands of Americans:* I was hard worked, ill fed, and well whipped. Mr. Stubbs, having once begun with me, did not suffer me to get over the effects of one whipping before he inflicted another. I have some marks of his about me which I expect to carry with me to the grave. All this time he assured me that what he did was only for my own good, and he swore that he would never give over until he had lashed my damned insolence out of me.

My life became unbearable. I wished for death. Nor do I know to what desperate actions I might have been driven had not one of those changes occurred to which a slave is ever exposed but over which he can exercise no control.

Colonel Moore, by the sudden death of a relation, inherited a large property in South Carolina. The deceased person had left a will about which there was a dispute which threatened to end in a lawsuit. The matter required Colonel Moore's personal attention, and he set out for Charleston, taking with him several of the servants. Mrs. Moore, soon after her husband's departure, sent for me to assist in filling up the gap which had been made in her domestic establishment.

I was truly happy at the change. I knew Mrs. Moore to be a lady who would never insult or abuse a servant unless she happened to be very much out of humor, an unfortunate occurrence which in her case did not happen oftener that once or twice a week—except, indeed, in very warm weather when the fit sometimes lasted for days together.

Shortly before this time, Miss Caroline, the Moore's older daughter, had returned from Baltimore, where she had been living for several years with an aunt who superintended her education. She was but an ordinary girl without much grace or beauty. But her maid, Cassandra—called Cassy—who had been born at Spring Meadow and had been sent off to the family connection in Baltimore when still a child, now returned a woman and was truly captivating. While in Baltimore, she had been trained as a lady's maid and she served Miss Caroline in that capacity.

Cassy was not tall—indeed, she was small—but the grace and elegance of her figure could not be surpassed. The vivacity of all her movements afforded a model which her languid and lazy mistress—who did nothing but loll all day upon a sofa—might have imitated to advantage. Cassy had a clear, soft, olive complexion and could boast a pair of black eyes which, for brilliancy and expression, I have never seen surpassed.

At this time I prided myself upon my color as much as did any white Virginian. Although I had found by bitter experience that a slave, whether white or black,

26

is still a slave, and that the master handles the whip with perfect impartiality—still, like my poor mother, I thought myself of a superior caste and would have felt it a degradation to put myself on a level with men a few shades darker than myself. This silly pride had kept me from forming intimacies with the other servants, either male or female, for I was decidedly whiter than any of them. It had, too, exposed me to an ill will among the slaves of which I had more than once felt the consequences, but which had not yet wholly cured me of my folly.

Cassy had more African blood than I. But this was a point which seemed of less consequence the more I became acquainted with her, and soon disappeared from my thoughts. We were much together because of our employment, and every day her beauty, vivacity, and good humor made a stronger impression upon me. I found myself in love before I had thought of it, and soon discovered that my affection was not unrequited.

Before long, we talked of marriage. Cassy consulted her mistress. The answer was favorable. Mrs. Moore listened with equal readiness to me. Women are never happier than when they have an opportunity to dabble a little in matchmaking, nor does the humble condition of the parties quite deprive the business of all its fascination.

A Sunday was fixed on as the day. A Methodist clergyman, one of those itinerant preachers who periodically wandered through the neighborhood arranging camp meetings for the religiously inclined, agreed to perform the ceremony. He was the more ready to do so for us because Cassy, while in Baltimore, had joined the

Methodists and had spent her Sundays in devoted attendance at a Negro Methodist congregation in that city.

That we were to be married in a small parlor of the master's house, with a minister of the church officiating, was for me a matter of immense pride and satisfaction. This is a measure of how white a black man I had become. The ceremony would proclaim in unmistakable terms, to whites and blacks alike, Cassy's and my inborn and undeniable superiority to the general run of blacks, who, it must be confessed, treat marriage as a matter of very little moment.

Marriage among slaves is far too often a temporary union; and the "blessed state of matrimony," as I heard it referred to at Colonel Moore's table, is contracted among slaves without any ceremony whatever. Slave "marriages" are given no recognition in law (for a slave can make no contract of any kind), are given no sanction nor regard whatever by masters, and as a natural result are often lightly esteemed by the parties concerned.

Indeed, how strange it would be to hear the solemn words "until death do you part" regularly pronounced over bowed black heads. For it is not so often the gleaning of the Grim Reaper that threatens to sunder the slave marriage. Too frequently it is murder by hate, by the slave driver's cruelty, by exhausting work coupled with poor nourishment, or the forced separation of the auction block, that breaks the marriage.

When at any time the husband can be sold into Louisiana, the wife into Georgia, there is slight inducement to draw tight the connubial bonds! And the joys of parenthood, too, are deprived the slaves, for their very children are regularly sold away from them. And if this most calamitous of events does not occur, the certainty that the fruits of their marriage, the children of their love, are to be born slaves and reared to all the privations and calamities of servitude, is enough to strike a damp into the hearts of the fondest couple.

Slaves, then, yield to the impulses of nature and propagate a race of slaves, but save in a few rare instances, slavery is as fatal to domestic love as it is to all other virtues. Some few choice spirits will rise superior to their condition and, when cut off from every other support, will find within their own hearts the means of resisting the deadly and demoralizing influences of servitude. In the same manner, yellow fever—while it rages through an infected city and sweeps its thousands and tens of thousands to the grave—finds here and there an iron constitution which defies its total malignity and sustains itself by the sole aid of nature's health-preserving power.

On the Friday before the Sunday which had been fixed upon for our marriage, Colonel Moore returned to Spring Meadow. His return was unexpected and, by me, very much unwished for. To the other servants who hastened to welcome him home, he spoke with his usual kindness and good nature. But though I had come forward with the rest of them, all the notice he took of me was a single glare of dissatisfaction. He appeared to be disagreeably surprised to see me again in the house.

The next day, just after the carriage rolled down the broad drive, carrying Colonel Moore, Miss Caroline, and my Cassy away for a call on neighbors, my mistress called me to her. She told me I was no longer needed as a house servant, that I should remove my possessions from the loft, and report at once to Mr. Stubbs.

This touched me to the quick. I carried my chest to the small hut that had earlier been assigned to Cassy and me, to be ours after our marriage. It was considerably better than Billy's and my hovel. It had a window and a rough floor, and was removed somewhat from the huts that formed "the town."

It as yet had no furniture whatever, but Cassy's eyes had glowed as she planned what it would be like after she set up housekeeping for us. She had enlisted the aid and active interest of her usually torpid mistress, who had promised certain articles from the big house. The promise that curtains would be forthcoming pleased Cassy so inordinately that I teasingly had pretended to believe that she was marrying me not for myself, but for the curtains. This brought my ardent Cassy flying into my arms, and I was the recipient of kisses and protestations of love, and vows that she would live with me in a cave or a hollow log—and a fig upon curtains!

My poor Cassy was to prove that her vows were the simple truth and would be kept almost to the letter.

Chapter 4

I reported to Mr. Stubbs and worked the day under his watchful eye. Well after sundown I circled the big house and the surrounding stables and collection of outbuildings, hoping for a chance to see Cassy, yet mindful that I must not be seen after dark anywhere on the plantation where I had not got permission to be. It was at length evident that her mistress was keeping her close and that she would have no opportunity to slip out in hope of meeting me. I went back to the hut and threw myself down, supperless, on the chest.

I cast about in my troubled mind as to the best way to approach Colonel Moore the next day, my wedding day, to beseech him to consider the unfitness of marriage between a lady's maid and a field hand, and to persuade him to admit me again to house service. I rehearsed over and over again the words I would say to him, and I practiced the deference, the humility, the respect, the *manner* of my presenting myself and my petition.

I was awake before first light, cooked a pot of meal to assuage my hunger, fetched a bucket of bath water from "the town" well, made my ablutions, arrayed myself in the good trousers and coat of the house servant, and a little before the time set for the wedding walked through the servants' entrance to the big house—the perfect picture of a groom ready and eager to claim his bride.

Once again I was confronted by Mrs. Moore, this time in a part of the house where she was seldom to be found, as if she had come there on purpose to intercept me. Such proved to be the case. She informed me that Colonel Moore, his daughter, and Cassy had again gone off in the carriage; that there was to be no marriage; that Miss Caroline had something better in mind for her little maid than marriage to a field hand.

I stumbled out much as a brute ox that has received a blow which has only barely failed to fell him. The few servants in the kitchen had remained busily at their light Sunday occupations, eyes lowered, giving every indication of being deaf and uncomprehending—the behavior expected of them.

Outside, I felt rather than saw that my black brothers had gathered closer to the house than was usual, lounged about in silent groups in Sunday idleness, and furtively watched me as I made my blind way to the cabin which was not now to be our bridal chamber.

Not one approached me in my stunned anguish, to console and commiserate with me, except Billy. As I approached the hut, he came out from the shadows of a grove of pines, put a hand on my arm, and halted my headlong pace.

He mentioned Colonel Moore. He mentioned Cassy's mother. I shook him off, calling him all kinds of a fool.

I shouted that Colonel Moore could burn in hell, and as for Cassy's mother, *she* could have no opinions of interest to me since she had been in her grave since Cassy was but four years of age! Billy got the full force of my profane vocabulary, which I had begun to acquire while attending the guests at Colonel Moore's drunken parties, and which had been enlarged and enriched since then by my schooling under Mr. Stubbs.

Billy was not such a dullard, poor fellow, as not to be able to see what stood before him, a most familiar sight: *a man colored white*, in the grip of an ungovernable rage unreasonably directed at him and threatening him with grave physical injury. He got out of my way.

In the blessed privacy of the cabin, I paced the floor, my mind searching for a way out of the catastrophe that had befallen me and my beloved. I would entertain one wild scheme, then another and another, only to discard all in turn. Toward afternoon I was physically exhausted and with this exhaustion came a quieting of my mind, allowing me to think of Cassy and of her plight. These thoughts led me to thoughts of the minister.

At once I went to seek out Mr. Stubbs, for permission to attend a camp meeting some five miles distant, where I knew the preacher to be holding forth. I would beg the parson—no matter what word he had had earlier about the cancellation of the wedding—to return to Spring Meadow and plead the cause of Cassy, his devout communicant.

Mr. Stubbs informed me that he had granted, earlier in the day, all the permissions for that particular camp meeting that he was going to grant; and what's more, he swore that he was tired of such gadding and had

33

made up his mind to grant no more passes for the next fortnight.

I had expected to get the pass, I suppose, yet this new evidence of Stubbs's petty tyranny did not surprise or provoke me. He had always been much opposed to all gadding. The wonder was that he had not before this adopted the measures of some "thrifty" managers and "good disciplinarians" whose policy was, and is, virtually to pen up their slaves when not at work, as they pen up their cattle, to keep them, as they say, out of mischief.

I returned to the cabin, and now my longing was to see Cassy. I lay on the chest, my head in my arms, and waited for nightfall and for the hour when Cassy would slip out of the big house. I knew that she would come—if not this night, then the next, and if not the next, then the one following or the one following that. I could take no untoward step to bring about the meeting, with-out endangering not only myself but her.

It was well past midnight. The moon had waned and soon would set, yet its light flooded the window and silvered the floor. The door opened—I had not heard her approach—and Cassy slipped in. I held her, sobbing, in my arms. I told her our hope lay in the preacher and begged her to get word to him.

She shook her head. "The master has made up his mind and is set against us. And he has nothing but hatred for preachers, especially the traveling, shouting kind. What are we to do, Archy? What can we do? We are lost!"

She pulled herself away, sank down on her knees beside the chest, and clasped her hands in an attitude of prayer. With her face lifted to the light of the moon, her cheeks glistening with traces of tears, she fervently beseeched God to come to our aid. In a moment she turned to grasp my hand and pull me down beside her. "Pray with me, Archy," she said.

I bowed my head and let her whispered entreaties serve for us both. I covered her hands, tightly clasped in prayer, with my own.

Her prayers ended, she raised her face to mine. Her dark and beautiful eyes were filled with the sadness of her despairing words. "Miss Caroline says she will make me happy, that she will find a husband for me."

My dear Cassy was disbelieving, dismayed. She had yet to learn of the contempt of the Negro that underlies slavery: which contempt, being absent, would render the institution of slavery unthinkable for the white man. Miss Caroline, of course, naturally subscribed to the prevailing opinion that black men and women were endowed with a singular appetite and aptitude for the physical expression of love, and totally bereft of the tender, more spiritual aspects of love between a man and a woman. Thus it was that she could (in all *innocence*, if I may use that word) shock and insult her young maidservant. **1614887**

"I shall marry no one, Archy, if not you," said my darling.

"You will marry me," I said. "Be my wife, Cassy."

Thus we were married, in the fashion of slaves everywhere in America, since we were slaves. I do not think that had twenty priests said a benediction over us and blessed our union, our vows would have been thereby

35

rendered more binding or our marriage more complete. Perhaps it might have been more secure.

It was impossible for my wife to visit me except by stealth, yet short and uncertain as these visits were, they sufficed to create and to sustain a new and singular state of feeling. My wife was seldom with me, but her image was ever before my eyes. The labor of the field was nothing; the brutality of the overseer was scarcely felt. My mind became so occupied with the pleasure which I found in our mutual affection that there was no room for disagreeable emotions. I was happy. Greater happiness I could not imagine and did not desire.

We had been married about a fortnight. It was near midnight, and I was sitting before my open door waiting for my wife to come (if she could come). The moon was high, the sky cloudless. As I gazed at the bright planet, I did not know myself to be a slave, destined to a servile condition on earth, but allowed my soul to soar and to feel the higher and nobler emotions of man's nature.

Presently I became aware that Cassy was coming. Failing to keep to the shadows of the trees, she hurried, skimming along the path, clearly visible in the patches of full moonlight that lay across her way. Alarm brought me to my feet. But, not to compound her recklessness, I held myself in the shadow of the cabin door until she came in, when with one movement I shut the door and took her into my arms. She shook uncontrollably, as with bone-chilling cold, and yet the night was warm. It was by slow degrees and in broken sentences that I learned the origin of her terror.

Colonel Moore had been paying her unusual attentions.

36

"I thought at first it was a father's kindness, Archy, because when I left Baltimore, Aunt Sarah said more than once that I was returning to my 'father's house' and that I would one day be a 'great lady.' But she is very old and addled; her mind wanders, and she is known for the stories she weaves to entertain the little children. Yet I had wondered lately if old Aunt Sarah may not have told the truth, and Colonel Moore my father. . . ."

She told me then in agonized whispers of the compliments he had paid her. He had sought her out to talk to her in a joking and teasing way, had remarked on her beauty, had at times stroked her cheek or her hair, and on occasion playfully pulled her against him, until at length she had to admit to herself that his words and actions hinted about a love that was not fatherly. She avoided him. She kept her distress from me, so as not to cloud our happiness, and prayed that his attentions, from lack of encouragement, would cease.

That hope had now vanished. When Mrs. Moore and Miss Caroline had gone calling on the neighbors in the afternoon, they had left Cassy at home. They had taken along to serve Miss Caroline a young slave girl who for the past week had been in the house to be trained as a lady's maid. This was not an unusual circumstance. Suitable subjects were often trained as servants, and if not needed in the house, were sure to fetch excellent prices when sold. Cassy had not looked on the girl as a threat to her own position. She had entered with good will into the training process and had herself instructed the girl in some of the rudiments of serving a mistress.

The ladies had been gone for some little time. Cassy was seated in Miss Caroline's room, engaged in needlework, when Colonel Moore entered. She rose hastily and would have gone out, but the master informed her that he had come expressly to talk to her. He told her that he had been unable to find a husband worthy of her, to take the place of "that scoundrel Archy," and that he had decided to take her himself.

He said this with a tone of tenderness which he no doubt meant to be irresistible. To many women in Cassy's situation, it would have been so. They would have felt flattered and honored. My mother had. . . .

"Oh, Archy, thank God, at least, that he is not my father. No father would—"

In this way Cassy had been able to decide that old Aunt Sarah was wrong. I was inclined to believe the contrary. I remembered most vividly how Billy had approached me, how he had linked Colonel Moore and Cassy's mother. I did not tell Cassy what I suspected to be the truth.

Our possible close blood ties made no difference to me. The nature of slavery makes incestuous alliances almost inevitable. We are known by one name only. We are encouraged to breed like common domestic animals. The masters know more of the bloodlines of their spirited racehorses than of their slaves! Slave mothers themselves are often unable to be certain who has fathered their children. To be born a man and a slave is to be born without a name or a history, the most degraded among humans. There is but one fate worse, and that is to be born a woman and a slave.

Cassy ended her recital by telling of the unexpected early return of the carriage and the abrupt end to the painful interview with Colonel Moore. The master had left Cassy with the injunction to dry her tears and to go greet her mistress with a smiling face. Her terror and dismay had stung him into a towering fury. He left her with the threat that they would talk another time; and that if she did not speedily choose to take advantage of his kind and generous offer to set her up in idleness and ease, as it was his pleasure to do, she would live to regret earning his displeasure.

Cassy felt that God had had a hand in the early return of the mistress, which return she felt had saved her from assault; for Colonel Moore was a victim of the lust he so contemptuously ascribed to his "savage" slaves. Unlike Cassy, I credited Mrs. Moore's return not to God, but to her own design.

Respectable wives of plantation owners are aware of the well-nigh irresistible temptation that the proximity and the helplessness of slave women have for their husbands and sons. They fight it while pretending ignorance of it. They know jealousy, humiliation, and despairing sorrow. They either, like the slaves themselves, turn to prayer and the certainty of happiness at last in heaven; or they allow the duplicity of their lives to sour their natures and render them subject to fits of temper, spiteful cruelties inflicted on defenseless victims, or frequent physical ailments of obscure origin.

Cassy said, "I cannot go back. I *cannot*! What is to become of us, Archy?"

My mind had long been made up. The slave in the extremity of affliction has but one poor and wretched recourse, to which he recurs always at the imminent risk of redoubling his miseries. That remedy is flight.

39

Chapter 5

We rolled into our blankets what cooking utensils we had accumulated, my allotment of corn and bacon, my good shirt and trousers, a hatchet, and other small articles that might prove useful. We considered Cassy's returning to the house for some of her possessions, but decided that the risk of detection and permanent separation was too great.

From under a loose floorboard we unearthed our pitiful little bag of coins, which I urged Cassy to conceal on her person. Some of these moneys I had accumulated by selling articles I had learned how to acquire, and which had a certain monetary exchange value among the slaves. Others had been pressed into Cassy's hand at various times by Miss Caroline. This not only demonstrated the young lady's kind generosity; it also provided her opportunities to remark that she wanted her little maidservant to indulge her amusing love of "baubles." This love of the gaudy and the frivolous is attributed to Negroes generally throughout the South.

We were soon ready. The time was well on toward

midnight. We had but a few hours to find cover, for it would not do to risk travel by daylight.

The fact that Colonel Moore did not keep hounds was in our favor. A man of the Colonel's sensibilities shrank from training bloodhounds on the place. His delicacy in the nefarious business of setting dogs on men did not, however, prevent his sending posthaste for the help of one of the neighbors whose sport and livelihood was the hiring out of himself and a vicious pack of well-trained dogs. But the time lost in assembling the hunt was time gained for Cassy and me, to put added miles between us and Spring Meadow.

We headed for a place I knew of, about ten to twelve miles distant by road. Its location was but hazy in my mind. I had been there on horseback with Master James, and on that occasion we had approached it by way of a weed-grown track leading off the main dirt road.

It was out of the question for Cassy and me to use the road. My plan was to strike off at a tangent in the hope that I would come upon the lower reaches of a brook which, if we followed it, would lead us to the spring that was its source. James and I had drunk at this spring. Our horses had slaked their thirst in its icy waters as it meandered through long grasses at the base of a steep ravine. On the higher ground above, at some distance from the brook, was situated the house and slave quarters of a long-abandoned plantation. On the occasion of our visit to the region we had skirted these ruins. It was known that the place was haunted.

Cassy and I struck off northwest, through woods, at a good pace. We spoke only when necessary and then in whispers. We skirted fields, keeping as much as possible

41

among trees and thickets. It was a difficult and tangled way, a zigzag course that added distance to our journey. At length Cassy grew tired—she was but ill-shod and poorly dressed for rugged travel—and so I supported her with one arm, and thus, somewhat more slowly, we continued. After hours of travel we broke out of a thicket to find ourselves on the bank of a river. I knew at once that we had traveled too far west. I vaguely surmised the abandoned plantation to be situated in a triangle between two rivers. To cross either of these would be an error.

Sensing my surprise, Cassy asked, "Are we lost?"

"No. Things could not be better for us. We will wade upstream, and here is where the hounds will lose us—if they trail us this far."

We took off our shoes; Cassy looped the hem of her skirt into the band about her slender waist; and we entered the water. The moon had paled. To our right the sky seemed to be lightening. Sleepy chirps in treetops announced that nature was awakening to a new day.

"Look for signs of a brook coming in from the right bank," I told Cassy. "We want to find the head of it."

Although I spoke confidently, I did not know that the brook emptied into this river. It might well drain into the other, many miles to the east. I kept these doubts to myself.

It was not by sight that we discovered the brook but by a change of temperature; the water about our ankles became perceptibly cooler. We halted, heard the faint splash and gurgle of running water, and at last noted the eddy of a brook from under a screen of tree branches, vines, and lush and rank water plants. We left the river and made our way up the swampy, overgrown bed of the choked waterway.

Day was long advanced when we reached the spring. We cooked a pot of meal, then rolled ourselves in our blankets and slept. Our exhaustion was extreme. It was imperative that we rest and restore our strength for the coming night's journey.

We awoke near sundown, and while we busied ourselves with our scanty evening meal, I thought over our situation. Cassy had no idea but that we would continue our flight north to freedom, but I had begun to have doubts about the wisdom of this. While we had traveled many weary miles, still—as the crow flies—we were no great distance from Spring Meadow. The folly of our remaining so close would be evident to all, and all would expect us to take advantage of our head start, to keep moving, in the hope of speedily putting ourselves out of reach. Dangerous as it was to remain so close, I persuaded myself that the greater folly would be to do the expected thing and thus risk flying straight into the arms of an aroused countryside.

Above the spring, and clinging to one side of the ravine, was a low brick building which Master James and I had discovered and explored. It was very much smaller than I remembered. It had once served as a dairy or cooling shed, or for some such purpose. One corner of the roof had fallen in. It had never had a window. Its door had long since fallen from its hinges, to rot and become part of the forest mold. This ruinous heap of bricks was shaded by several ancient trees, and more recent growth so crowded it as to render it practically invisible.

43

Cassy and I explored the ravine in the fading light. We scrambled up its steep sides and found ourselves on the edge of what had once been one of the extensive fields of the plantation. An impenetrable thicket covered the whole of this cursed place, which well deserved its fate. Had the soil been cultivated by free men it might still be producing rich and abundant harvests. But the owner was one of those who had neither skill nor taste for husbandry. It was characteristic of untold numbers of ignorant and rapacious planters that they flailed their land as they flailed their human charges, in the expectation of having but seven to ten years to "get the good" out of them. Ruination of both was the inevitable result.

The plantation house and surrounding buildings could not be seen from where Cassy and I stood. The house had been standing when Master James and I had caught fearful sight of it, perhaps held precariously upright by the creeping vines that covered it. At that time the courtyard would not have been known as such, so overgrown was it with young trees. The scene then had been one of utter silence and desolation; little wonder that my young brother and I had fled it as malevolent, cursed, and haunted! And neither would Cassy and I go near it, for search parties might easily wander up the lane from the main road and sniff about there for runaways.

We decided to go to ground at the base of the ravine, the brick structure there to serve as our home. Pine boughs heaped in a corner of this place served as our bed. And, rude as our life there was, we were happy. As day followed summer day, we felt increasingly more safe. We exulted in our new-found freedom and in our love. We were safe, although almost in the center of

44

civilization, and we were safe for the reason that no one supposed us to be so foolish as to be where we were.

There were several plantations about, for lowlands along the two rivers were still in cultivation, but to my knowledge there was no house nearer than Spring Meadow. I spent many a night foraging the countryside for roasting ears, just coming to maturity. I traveled to the river after dark and never failed to net us a nice catch of fish before daylight. I found my rude rabbit trap empty more often than I found a rabbit in it, but we enjoyed roast rabbit on more than one occasion. The fruit we picked from trees at the edge of a grove long reverted to a wild state was scarce and of inferior quality. We declared it delicious.

Many were the daylight hours I spent in that blessed retreat, in complete idleness. I used to lie for hours in a dreamy sort of indolence, outstretched upon the shady slope, enjoying the sweet consciousness that I was free, my own master, and luxuriating in the knowledge that I need come or go at no one's bidding, would work or not work according to my own good will.

Are emancipated slaves inclined to indolence, as is said? If so, let no one wonder at it. Labor, in their minds, is indissolubly associated with servitude and the whip; and *not to work*, they have ever been taught, is the badge and peculiar distinction of freedom. I gave myself up to the delight of doing nothing—for hours on end.

We lay hidden for well over a month and at last felt sure that the first hue and cry of the search had died down and that the time had come to set out for the North.

We decided that we should travel as poor whites,

down on our luck and out to seek our fortunes, and that Cassy must be clothed as a boy. We counted over our store of coins which we had hoped to have for expenses on the road, but which now must, in part, be spent for clothing for Cassy.

There was no slave at Spring Meadow whom I could seek out to ask to steal or to buy the needed articles. Nay, were there any at Spring Meadow who catching sight of me would not give the alarm? Why would they not when by so doing they could hope for favored treatment from Mr. Stubbs, if only by a more generous indulgence in Sunday passes? There was no one in the whole countryside who would extend me the hand of friendship in my extremity.

But there was one, a white man, who owed me a favor. I had, he swore, saved his life. A worthless life, it is true, but of value to him, to judge by the small presents he sometimes pressed into my hand, and his frequent retelling of the incident to all who would listen.

He had been fishing when a sudden squall had upset the boat. He could swim after a fashion; but panic seized him, and his frantic cries for help as he floundered toward the shore of the lake, and his frequent sinking beneath the waves, whipped up by the wind, made it likely he would never reach it. I was fourteen or fifteen at the time. I plunged in, swam out to him, and got an arm about his neck and towed him to shore. He was by then nearly unconscious. There was no panic or fight left in him, or the tale might well have ended differently. This man was one Jemmy Gordon.

He kept a little store, his principal customers the slaves of neighboring plantations. He was of that order

46

known as *poor white trash,* of which there are considerable numbers in Virginia. He had neither land nor servants, for his father before him had been a poor man. He had been educated to no trade. Where every planter has his own slave mechanics on his plantation, working oftimes with great skill *for no wage,* there is no incentive for a white man to learn the mechanic arts.

Jemmy Gordon had somehow scraped together the little capital needed to set himself up as a trader. He, of course, traded in a very small way. He dealt principally in whiskey. In addition, he kept shoes, some clothing, and such household articles as slaves need to eke out the miserable and insufficient supply they receive from their masters. He was often forced to accept corn and other produce in payment, without making any inquiry as to how his black customers came into possession of it.

Though trade with slaves is dangerous and disgraceful, and the traders in consequence are desperate and reckless, they still flourish in numbers so great as to furnish the planters with an inexhaustible topic for declamation and complaint. And these planters tell the simple truth when they complain that the traders accept stolen goods in place of legal tender. It is in vain that tyranny fences itself about with the terrors of the law. It is in vain that the slaveholder flatters himself with the hope of appropriating, to his own sole use, the entire fruits of the forced labors of his fellow men. Fraud is the natural counterpart of tyranny. Cunning is ever the defense of the weak against the oppressions of the strong.

Can the unhappy slave who has been compelled to plant in the daytime for his master's benefit, be blamed

47

if he strives in the night to gather some gleaning of the crop for his own use? Blame him, you who can!

Why, this same master who sees no wrong in robbing slaves of their labor—their sole possession and only earthly property!—this man himself carries the art of pillage to a perfection of which robbers and pirates never dream! The debased slave snatches such casual spoils as chance and cunning make possible; but the slaveholder, whip in hand, extorts from his victims a large, regular, rich, and annual plunder, *and demands the right to transmit to his children, under law, this privilege of systematic pillage!*

My one hope lay, then, in this trader, this Jemmy Gordon.

Chapter 6

It was after midnight when I approached his house and store, both under the same roof, situated at a lonely crossroads. I stepped on the stoop and knocked. I had knocked a second time before Jemmy Gordon thrust his head from a window and asked what I wanted.

"Let me in, Jemmy," I said, turning so that the moonlight fell full on my face. His head disappeared from the window; the door opened enough to let me through, and closed behind me.

"My God, Archy, is it you? Where have you sprung from? It's been said for a month that you'd got clean away!"

I told him I had not, but that I meant to and that I needed his assistance.

"Anything in reason, Archy—"

"What I need are some articles of clothing, and information on the road I should take."

"You saved my life, boy, and one good turn deserves another. That's what I say. But this is a damned bad business. Why the devil must you and that wench be running away? I never knew any mischief in my life that a woman wasn't at the bottom of it!"

I told him that running away wasn't the question. We had done it. Now the thing was for us not to be taken again, and I relied on his help.

"You listen to me, Archy!" he said, excitedly. "It's the wench that the Colonel is most angered about. Better make up your minds to go in, take your whippings, and make the best of it. If you was to go in, Archy—make a merit of telling where your master could find her—I'm bound you would get off easy in the end."

I choked down my indignation. Jemmy Gordon could not be expected to rise above current morals, nor could he imagine that I might not share them. I hinted that I had money to pay for all I wanted and would not dispute about the price. Was it this last hint, or some more generous motive, that caused him to exhibit a more favorable disposition?

"As to money, Archy, between friends like us there is no need of speaking about that. But you'll never get off. Mind what I tell you, you'll never get off! The Colonel's got handbills stuck up all through the country. I'll show you. It's *five hundred dollars reward* he's got posted!"

He lighted a candle and led me through a door into the store. He held the flame close to the notice posted on the wall. The big reward was printed in suitably large letters at the top, followed by our descriptions. I was said to be about twenty-one years of age, six feet or better in height, muscular frame, erect walk, "hair a deep brown and curls over his head, eyes blue, high forehead," and "smiles when spoken to." Cassy was described as about eighteen, five feet and three inches in

50

height, long black hair, and "a very bright black eye. Makes handsome appearance. Has a good voice and can sing several songs. Both runaways are very light colored and will try to pass. Thought likely to be making for Baltimore."

We turned away from the handbill. Jemmy Gordon took out a bottle of whiskey and poured generous drinks for us both.

"There you have it, Archy, a bad business." He downed his whiskey and poured himself another. "I'll help you, if your mind's made up. But you'll never get away, mark my words, Archy! And don't give out where your help came from, when they've got you back!"

He thrust the candle into my hand and waved an arm, indicating the few bins and shelves that constituted his store. "Pick out what you want," he said.

I hurriedly collected caps and shoes for both Cassy and me. There was no boy's clothing. Mr. Gordon said he would collect trousers and a shirt from some other trader and have the articles for me the next night. There was nothing for me to do but to make the best of this setback. I heaped what I had on the table and asked him what I owed.

He took his slate and began to figure it up. He proceeded diligently for a few minutes, then came to a full stop. He looked at the goods I had selected, then at the slate. He hesitated, glanced up at me, and said, "Archy, you saved my life. You're welcome to them 'ere things, by God!"

Since we were expected to try to go to Baltimore, I got from Jemmy information on all roads except the one to Baltimore.

51

"Archy, I'll be off drinking with some gentlemen to-morrow night. I'll leave the window off the latch and what I can scrounge for you will be stacked under it, handy. And see you leave the window closed like you found it."

I thanked him, hastily gathered up my "purchases," and left. My presence was a great danger to him and I knew he wanted nothing more than to see the last of me.

Cassy stayed concealed in the woods a little distance from Jemmy's place the next night while I cautiously approached. I stood in the shadows for some time, watching and listening. There seemed at last no doubt but that Jemmy had deserted the place and that no stray wayfarer was on either of the roads that crossed there.

I moved in stealthily, raised the window with utmost quietness, threw a leg over the sill, and hunched over to enter.

"Seize him! Seize him!"

It was Stubbs who yelled. Other voices joined his. The building burst with shouts and curses. Hands were laid on me. I jerked out of their grasp and toppled backward out of the window, but not before a pistol ball was sent to the target I made in the window square. It nearly accomplished its purpose. It grazed my skull, stunning and deafening me.

I fell but, stunned or not, got to my feet and ran like a drunken man, crying out to Cassy to flee. Then I caught sight of her running among the trees and not away but toward me. Pistol balls racketed about us. I lurched toward Cassy, threw her to the ground, my body shielding hers. The poor girl was out of her mind with terror and wildly crying. I believe I, too, sobbed; and if so, was it in terror or because we had for the moment escaped death? Something there is in humans that values life and will hold fast to the precious gift. Even the most lowly have this instinct to live—even slaves.

I was either dazed by my head wound or had learned well the lesson of the slave. I made no resistance when they fell upon me, made my hands fast, and put a collar and chain about my neck. I was aware that similar treatment was given to the weeping and near-fainting Cassy, that she was roughly handled, and I made no outcry. I made no outcry when the foul-mouthed Stubbs directed coarse and brutal remarks to her, aided and urged on by the three or four other roustabouts who crowded around.

It was Jemmy who unexpectedly came to her assistance. He took charge, saying it was he who had made the arrangements with the Colonel; it was he who would collect the reward; and the bargain was that the two runaways should be brought in alive and well—or, if not, the reward would be cut in half. And he told them all that the whiskey he had promised them for their part in the night's fun would be cut at least by half if his own reward became less as a result of their "damn fool shenanigans."

I was not able to walk or talk with Cassy. She was sent on with Stubbs and two others. The remaining two stayed with me and Jemmy, who told them to remain some paces behind as he wanted to have a few private words with me.

My wound bled profusely; my head throbbed to bursting, and there was a humming in my ears. Yet something of what the traitor Gordon said to me as he walked beside me (even, sometimes, reaching a steadying hand to me when I stumbled!), something of his whining excuses, sank into my mind.

He had decided to collect the reward, for why in the name of God should he let it slip through his fingers? And all for nothing, too, because he knew right well I would be taken and someone else collect the prize that could be his. Yet, because I had saved his life, he had gone to the Colonel early that day and had said "if he could bring Archy and the wench in, would the Colonel leave off the whippings, because Archy had saved his life once and he would on *no account* bring him in if he was to be whipped!" To seal the bargain, Jemmy had offered to accept a lesser reward—a mere four hundred and fifty dollars.

The fellow said, in an aggrieved tone, that I should "take it more kindly." He said that he had done "what was best for the both of us." Because of him, he said, I was to get off lightly for running off with the likeliest wench at Spring Meadow, and one the Colonel meant for himself, as any fool could see. I should thank my lucky stars, said Jemmy Gordon.

Now what of this great bargain my friend had struck for me with Colonel Moore, the honorable *Virginia gentleman*? Why, the gentleman's code is understood among these gentlemen not to extend to contemptible white trash, whom they hold to be little better than ignorant blacks. I was strung up, and Stubbs laid on forty lashes, not all of which I felt, for I lost consciousness before the half had been delivered.

The reader may think it remarkable that I can say

54

here that Jemmy Gordon was not a completely depraved man. He had a conscience, small and weak as it was, or else why would he have approached the master with talk of bargains and leniency? It must be remembered that the sum of five hundred dollars was a great temptation to Jemmy Gordon. Almost equally tempting was the chance of gaining favor with Colonel Moore, whose good will would help Jemmy's ambition of gaining a place of comfortable respectability in the region. The desire for respectability is a positive disease among Americans of all classes and colors.

Nowhere in the world is the distinction between gentlemen and common people more distinctly marked than in slaveholding America. Gentlemen there consider it an insult to be compared with the likes of Jemmy Gordon. Yet their whole lives are a continued practice of the "principles" on which that man acted. The Jemmy Gordons can take lessons in lying, deceit, and self-deception from the respectable and superior Southern gentlemen.

Many are the gentlemen in slaveholding America who know full well that to keep their fellow man in bondage is a practice, abstractly considered, more criminal than piracy or highway robbery. The slaveholder acknowledges to himself and to others that slavery, in the abstract, is totally indefensible. But then, his slaves are his estate! He cannot live in gentlemanly idleness without them. Besides, he treats them particularly well. When looked at rightly, it can be seen that he is doing the wretches a favor, for they are much happier as slaves than freedom, under any form whatever, could possibly make them! These gentlemen have talked themselves into an unshakable belief that slavery is best for both slaveowner and slave.

When men of sense and education can satisfy themselves with such wretched sophistry as this, let us summon up some charity for the likes of the despicable Jemmy Gordon.

I lay on a wretched pallet in a dark, airless cell, which had been built in the corner of one of the stables for the express purpose of holding dangerous rebels among the slaves. I believe I was close to death at this time and that my death was expected and hoped for. For a period of a week or ten days, I lay there feverish and delirious. I remember hallucinations about the spring in the ravine and of drinking that cold, sweet water and of its cascading all over me. In my imaginings, Cassy, who had our money concealed in a hidden pocket of her skirt, took out the little bag, which had become large and fat, and from it she poured a cascade of golden coins, and I heard her laugh, a laugh as musical as falling water. I understood from this that Cassy had been able to buy her freedom and was happy.

These fantasies were my medicine (for I believe that none other was given me), and they were curative. They quieted my fevered brain and allowed my body to rest and heal itself. At last I awoke one day, very weak but with a clear head. I realized where I was and saw that I was in charge of a deaf old crone. It was some time in that dim place before I could get her attention, by making signs, and beg for water. She gave me some.

I was later able to take food and still later, always after dark, allowed to walk about among the barns for half an hour or so for exercise. Peter, a black man and one of Mr. Stubbs's most trusted assistants, put the collar and chain on me and accompanied me on these excursions. He would tell me nothing of Cassy's fate, and at length I gave up asking. I came to believe that Mistress Caroline had sorely missed her little maid's solicitous attentions, had decided to blame Cassy's bad behavior entirely on me, and had entreated Colonel Moore to take her back into the family on the old terms. It gave me great comfort to believe this. I was grateful that she was to be spared punishment and that I was to be allowed to take hers along with my own.

Stubbs came into my cell one day, tossed a worn shirt and trousers down, and told me to put them on early the next morning and be prepared to travel. I asked him where I was going. He did not reply even to the extent of indulging himself in his usual string of oaths.

Ostracism is one of the more refined and piercing of the cruelties everywhere practiced in the South. To ask even the simplest question and get no answer, as if you had not spoken; to stand forward only to be brushed aside as if in fact you were not there, can convince even a rational man of the irrationality of supposing his own existence. Such, at least, has been my experience.

It was still dark when Stubbs and I set out in the morning. He traveled ahead on a good horse, saddled and well equipped with the trappings of the traveler. I rode bareback on one of the work animals. My hands were bound together, but loosely enough to grasp the mane of the animal, to steady myself if the need arose. A rope tied about my neck was secured at the other end

57

about the waist of Mr. Stubbs. I did not need to ask where we were going. Stubbs was taking two animals to public auction.

That night we stayed at a sort of tavern, a run-down and noisome place—he on the bed, I on the floor. The end of the rope was taken from about Stubbs's waist and tied so tightly about my ankles that I could not sleep for pain. The next morning my feet were so painfully swollen and tender, I could scarcely stand. Stubbs cursed and said I should have let him know. I said nothing. I can still recall with great clarity how he had lain on the bed the preceding night, slightly propped up on a pillow, his whip laid out alongside him, ready to hand. Had I complained, interrupting his rest, the whip would have silenced me.

Late that evening we entered the city of Richmond. I was taken at once to the city jail and locked up for safe-keeping.

Chapter 7

I had never been in a city the size of Richmond. I had never attended a slave auction, having known only of a sale or two at Spring Meadow that had been arrived at by private treaty. I recall but a few incidents from the Richmond auction. My mind was too numbed with exhaustion and despair to be able to take in the whole noisy, exciting scene.

I was chained and fettered, which was to be expected. But I was puzzled that an elderly man and a girl of about twelve were chained together. Tears streaked the faces of both. Perhaps they were grandfather and granddaughter. The age of the man and the youth of the girl should have made such precautions against their escape unnecessary, so perhaps the heavy and degrading chaining of these two weak creatures was meant as extra punishment, rather than security.

A man and his wife—she with an infant in her arms— seemed terrified of being separated. The woman hurried up to one of the spectators and begged him to buy both herself and her husband; and she enumerated with great

59

volubility the good qualities of each. The man so entreated looked on the ground and preserved a moody and sullen silence, while the poor woman cast her glances about, anxious to find a purchaser who seemed to indicate some interest in buying her little family unit.

Do not imagine that all was wailing and weeping. A group of eight or ten men and women laughed and talked spiritedly. They were almost gay. Apologists for tyranny rejoice in such a scene and find in it an argument that, after all, being sold at public auction is not so terrible a thing as some weak people are apt to imagine. The argument is quite as sound as any that the slaveholder ever uses. The truth is that the human mind in its eager struggle after happiness will, even in the valley of despair, strive to create some matter of enjoyment. The poor slave will sing at his task. He can laugh, too, though he finds himself sold like an ox in the market. When the tyrants discover that their wrongs and oppressions have not been able to extinguish the God-given capacity for enjoyment in the souls of their victims, they dare boast of the happiness tyranny causes! "These are happy brutes" say the sellers of slaves. Has any horse auctioneer ever offered a group of "happy horses" for sale? Happiness and the pursuit of happiness are characteristic only of the human animal. On this point alone, the slaveholder's argument—that *man* can be bought and sold and worked as a common beast of burden—is shown to be a self-serving lie.

My bruised senses were afflicted anew by what I witnessed that day. A dashing and buckish young man was put up. A gentleman from the neighborhood was bidding, and the voluble young slave kept urging him on,

60

calling upon him by name, entreating him to buy. He didn't want to be sent away from the neighborhood. Yet whenever a second bidder, a slave trader from South Carolina, raised the bid, the poor slave saw the danger of offending a man who might become his master, so he was at pains to say that he knew the bidder was a fine gentleman but that he was a stranger and would take him away from his wife and children. And here the slave would start all over again his entreaties to the local gentleman, and not even the whip could keep him still.

I was put up. Stubbs walked off and sat at some distance, chewing and spitting tobacco, the very picture of indifference, although sometimes I caught a squinted look from him sent in my direction. He made no effort to point out my good qualities. At the time I was not aware of the implications of this, but I believe that it was Colonel Moore's intention that I should go cheap, as a final cruelty. An ambition common among slaves is to bring a high price. This is the last and lowest form in which is displayed that love of superiority which is the mainspring of human action, the source of all social improvements, and the origin of so much crime and misery.

The auctioneer did his best. I was strong, a good laborer, docile and obedient, or so he assured the skeptical audience.

I had been stripped half-naked. I was whirled about, my limbs were felt; my capabilities discussed in a slang much like that of a company of horse jockeys. The auctioneer had said I was strong; I was obviously a set of bones wrapped in a scarred and filthy skin. He had said

61

I was docile; the onlookers said I had a damned sullen look. One said I was clearly consumptive. Another said I didn't have enough nigger in me to be worth anything and that the lighter ones were the worst kind.

I paid no attention to the human vultures punching and pinching and turning me about. I didn't care what became of me, until a voice spoke up, challenging the auctioneer.

"A docile fellow, you say! Look at that back! He got those stripes for docility, did he, sir?"

"Proof positive that he's docile—now! He's been well broke, as you can see," said the auctioneer.

"It's a damned disgrace!" This from a man on the platform. I turned to see a portly, round-faced gentleman, his face quite pink with anger.

I mumbled, "I'm a trained house servant, sir. I can read and write, sir."

He stumped off the platform. A few others came up for a closer look and the opportunity to make a few remarks. The bidding started. It was far from spirited. I kept my gaze on the portly gentleman. His face remained pink. His ire was up. I believe he would have paid a high price for me, but that was not necessary. He got me cheap.

He at once told the auctioneer to knock off my irons. There was an outcry from the auctioneer and several others.

"Unchain him at your own risk!" they said. "He's a mean one and a smart one. He'll run off the first chance he gets."

To this, the man (who had announced himself as Major Thornton) replied contemptuously that his slaves never wanted to run away, but that if any gave signs of wanting to, he sold them off at once. "No slave works for me who don't *want* to work for me," he said.

I had never heard such an opinion expressed. It struck me as exceedingly novel and made Major Thornton an interesting individual in my eyes.

My new master procured a horse for me, and we set out together, riding side by side, another novel experience for a slave. He talked constantly as we traveled, and I soon realized that he was an eccentric. Not the least of his eccentricities was that although he owned and operated a plantation, he did not call himself a planter but a farmer.

Major Thornton lived a considerable distance west of Richmond in that part of the state known as middle Virginia. It was dusk before we arrived at Oakland, as his property was called. The main house was not large, but it was neat and very handsome, and presented many more appearances of substantial comfort than were to be found about most of the houses I had seen in Virginia. At a distance were the servants' cabins, built of brick as was the main house, and not placed in a straight line but clustered together in a manner that had something picturesque about it. They were shaded by fine large oaks. Neither underbrush nor weeds were suffered to grow about them. I was struck by the contrast to the long line of ill-kept hovels that comprised "the town" at Spring Meadow. And here at Oakland the children were dressed, rather than running about naked or half-naked; and the hands, who were just coming in from their work, were all well clothed. Not one was arrayed in the expected rags and tatters.

The stock of slaves at Oakland numbered upwards of eighty. Forty of them were working hands, and the balance were the children and the elderly. The Major kept no overseer but managed for himself. He said that an overseer was enough to ruin any man.

In this opinion, and in many others, he was very different from his neighbors. He was too individual for their tastes, and he was little liked by any of them. He avoided horse races, cockfights, political meetings, drinking, gambling, and frivolity of every sort. His neighbors revenged themselves for this contempt of their favorite pastimes by pronouncing him a mean-spirited, money-making fellow. They even went so far as to suggest that he was a bad citizen and a dangerous neighbor. They complained that his excessive indulgence of his servants made all the slaves in the neighborhood uneasy and discontented, and that if there were to be a slave uprising in the community, it would be the Major's fault! Some favored giving him a stiff warning to mend his ways or move out of the county.

The Major had been born of a good family, as they say in Virginia, but when he was a mere boy, his father died and left but a very scanty property. He began his adult life in a very small way in a small-town store. His shrewdness, economy, and attention to his business enabled him to lay up a considerable sum of money. When Oakland came on the market (to pay off the debts of a profligate owner), Major Thornton was able to buy it.

Major Thornton did not grow tobacco. His principal crop was wheat, and he was a great advocate of the clover system of cultivation, whereby he periodically rested and restored his fields by sowing them in clover,

64

a plan which he adopted and pursued with much success. The planters roundabout had looked on in astonishment at the renovation in the buildings and the increase in soil fertility brought about at Oakland after my master became the owner. They wondered how it could possibly happen.

He did not hesitate to explain it all to them, for he was extremely fond of talking about himself, his philosophy in general, and his system of farming. As far as I know, he was never able to make a convert. He never could persuade these traditional planters that clover was the true cure for sterile fields; that the only way to have a plantation well managed was for the owner to manage it himself; and that to give servants enough to eat was a sure method for preventing their plundering of cornfields and stealing of sheep.

In no respect was the Major more an innovator than in the management of his slaves. A merciful man, he used to say, was merciful to his beast, and he could not bear the idea of treating his servants worse than his horses. As for whipping, Major Thornton "could not stomach it." Whether he felt some qualms of conscience at the tyranny of the lash, or whether it was the influence of that instinctive humanity which will not permit us to inflict pain without ourselves feeling a sympathetic suffering, or whatever else might be the reason, Major Thornton certainly had a great horror of the lash.

Evidence of a brutal use of the lash on me must certainly be counted the moving force in his bidding for me at the Richmond sale, and not, as in my pride I had imagined, the fact that I was a trained house servant and could read and write. When I became his property,

65

however, astute manager that he was, he made use of such talents as I had. I became a favorite and a very useful addition to his household staff.

Yet my new master was (what every other slaveholder is, and from the very necessity of his condition must be) a tyrant. He felt no scruple in compelling his fellow man to labor in order that he might appropriate the fruits of that labor. Is it not just in this that the very essence of tyranny exists? My master was, then, a tyrant, but as reasonable and humane a one as the system and his own nature allowed.

Major Thornton was as ready as his neighbors to denounce the idea of emancipating the slaves. The notion of freeing his servants or of limiting his power over them he considered an absurdity, "an impertinent interference with his most sacred rights." He did not maintain power by the whip but through a different terror. If one of his servants were guilty of anything which in a slave is esteemed especially reprehensible, such as attempting escape, repeated theft, idleness, drunkenness that interfered with work, or insubordination, Major Thornton sent the offender to the auction block. By some strange inconsistency he felt no scruples at all at tearing a man from his wife and children, setting him up at public sale, pocketing a good profit, and allowing the wretch to fall into the hands of any ferocious master who might chance to purchase him. This dread of being sold away from a good master, one whom most of us at Oakland regarded with real devotion, was very efficacious in keeping us at home.

Besides, we were safer at home. Plantation owners, overseers particularly, and common white trash, too,

66

took a positive delight in abusing the slaves of Major Thornton when they found them abroad. Consequently, we did not wander. And since Major Thornton professed no interest in what we did in our off-hours on the plantation, and since he did not care how much we drank (so long as it did not interfere with our work), the slaves spent many an evening and most of Sunday drinking, dancing, singing, playing games of chance, and in all ways disporting themselves as if they were free men and masters of their fate!

I spent most of my time with Major Thornton. He loved a listener, and I had no objection to playing the role. On occasion I joined the other slaves in their frolics but did not feel comfortable with them. I had been too long unsociable to be able to acquire the art easily. I much preferred to drink by myself and often tramped about the place at night, nipping from a flask, thinking about Cassy and about Major Thornton, and wondering if it might not be possible, when I knew the man better, to tell him about my wife and beg him to buy her and bring her to Oakland. I more and more frequently resorted to the bottle to conjure up in a liquor-inflamed imagination these wild dreams of happiness for Cassy and me. Drunkenness, which degrades the free man to a level with the brutes, raises, or seems to raise, the slave to the dignity of a man. It soon became my one sure pleasure, and I indulged it to excess.

One Sunday I had been drinking until I was no longer master of my own actions. I foolishly wandered out of the woods and down the road with some destination in mind, I know not what. I at length stumbled, lost my balance, and fell down on the carriageway leading to the main house, and there I lay. After some time I came to my senses and tried to rise. At almost the same instant I saw approaching two neighboring planters, come to call on Major Thornton.

They, also, had undoubtedly been drinking. When they saw me, my difficulty in rising, and the helpless position I was in, they saw a prime opportunity for jollity and sport. They took it into their heads to jump their horses over me. One put spurs to his mount and brought him up to the leap, but the horse shied at sight of me, reared back, and threw the rider. The other gentleman leaped from his horse to capture the loose animal and to help his friend to his feet.

I continued to lie there as if insensible. My danger, however, had considerably sobered me. The neighbors discussed my disgraceful drunken condition, remarking that if they had come upon me off Thornton's property they would have whipped some decency into me, and made this an occasion to remark on the Major's idiocy in allowing drinking among the niggers.

"Makes them stupid and easy to manage, so he says," one of them said sarcastically.

The other gentleman, mimicking the Major, said, "A drunk one can't run good, can't run far. Easy to catch."

They mounted their horses and, full of their contempt and bursting with the tale they would tell my master as soon as they reached the house, cantered away.

My mind had cleared sufficiently for me to be able to understand the full import of what I had just heard. The brief conversational exchange had given me new insight into Major Thornton's character and his theories of slave management. I was not yet so far lost as to be able to endure the idea of being myself the instrument of my own destruction. I determined to get drunk no more, and have not been drunk since.

Chapter 8

Some persons, perhaps, may think that having fallen into the hands of such a master as Major Thornton, I had now nothing to do but to eat, sleep, attend my master, and be happy. Had I been a horse or an ox there would be good ground for this idea. But I was a man, and the animal appetites are by no means the only spur to human action or the sole source of human happiness or misery. I was perhaps more indulged than any servant on the place, but this could not make me happy.

Human happiness, with some very limited exceptions, is never in fruition but always in prospect and pursuit. It is not this, that, or the other situation that can give happiness. Riches, power, glory, are nothing when possessed. Happiness lies in the pleasure of pursuit, the struggle for attainment.

Those moralists who have declaimed so copiously on the *duty of contentment* betray an extreme ignorance of human nature. No situation, however splendid, in which one is compelled to remain fixed and stationary can long afford pleasure. On the other hand, no destitute or degraded condition out of which one has anything like a rational hope of rising can be justly considered as utterly miserable. This is the constitution of the human mind. In this we find the explanation of a thousand things which, without this key to their meaning, seem full of mystery and contradiction.

Though all men have not the same objects of pursuit, all are impelled by the same love of pursuing. Nothing can satisfy the vast desires of one man but immense wealth or great political power. Another aims no higher than to rise from abject poverty to a little competency. A third has an ambition of another sort—to be the chief personage in his native village or the oracle of a country neighborhood. How different are these aims!—and yet the impulse that prompts them is the same.

He whom circumstances permit to yield to this impulse of his nature and to pursue (whether successfully or not matters little)—but to pursue with some tolerable prospect of success—the objects which have captivated his fancy may be regarded as having all the chance for happiness which the lot of humanity allows. He who is compelled, by fate, fortune, or whatever malignant cause, to forego the instinctive impulses and wishes of his heart is a wretch entitled to the greatest pity. To the one, toil is itself a pleasure; desire sustains him; and hope cheers him on. These are pleasures the other never knows. For him life has lost its relish; rest is irksome to him; labor is intolerable.

It is true that my situation was far superior to that of many free men. But I lacked one thing which every free man has, and that one lack of mine was enough to make me miserable. I wanted liberty. I wanted the liberty of laboring for myself, not for a master, and of pursuing my own happiness instead of toiling for another's pleasure and for his gain. This liberty can lighten the hardest lot. He knows but little of human nature who has not discovered that it is far pleasanter for a man to starve and freeze after his own fashion than to be fed and clothed and forced to work under another's compulsion.

In my delirium at Spring Meadow I had imagined Cassy free and happy. In my alcoholic maunderings at Oakland I had imagined my kind master bringing us together to live in bliss, perhaps with our own little children about us. But in the sober Sundays following my determination not to drink, I saw that even if Major Thornton, as intermediary, accomplished all this, our happiness would depend on his continued favor. In all this I saw that I had no choice but the choice between greater or lesser evils. I was a victim of the worst evil—slavery—and from slavery Major Thornton would not free me and my beloved.

Since my life depended upon his caprice, I studied the man. I came to think that his humanity might more correctly be seen as a sense of his own interest. His humanity preserved his slaves from hunger and nakedness, but exposed them to other excruciating miseries.

Consider this, that we were denied the necessity and excitement of plunder! In this we were denied the exercise of our ingenuity and an object in which to interest ourselves. The opportunity for plans and stratagems in our own behalf was denied us.

Then, again, our master allowed each of us a little piece of ground. This was customary in those parts. What was contrary to custom was that he allowed us time to cultivate our crops, then purchased all we could produce, and at a fair price. The Thornton slaves had honestly earned coins jingling in their pockets and were given the inestimable privilege of spending them as they pleased. Our choice of commodities to buy was an extremely narrow one, however, and the result was that we became a set of drunkards. Sunday was generally a grand Saturnalia.

It was thoughts such as these that made me hesitate to expose the deepest desire of my heart to Major Thornton. If he could not see at once that what was in my interest was also in his own, my petition could easily be twisted into an example of outrageous insolence and impertinence.

Was what will be seen as my distrust of this seemingly good man not excessive and self-defeating? Perhaps. Yet when I had been with him less than a year, and while wrestling with my anxieties concerning him, this proud, independent, unpredictable man of eccentric views and quarrelsome temper met his death as the result of these very qualities in his nature.

The tale is soon told. I had been sent on a Saturday to deliver an intemperate note to Captain Robinson about his neglect of lower-field fences that bordered on Major Thornton's property. These two men had such frequent altercations that one is tempted to believe they deliberately concocted them because of a perverse enjoyment of them.

On the following day I was passing along on the public road when I met Captain Robinson on horseback, followed by his manservant, Matt. He reined in his horse and demanded if I were the damned rascal who had delivered Thornton's note to his overseer. I replied, "Yes, sir."

"And a damned insolent message it was, by God! If my overseer had known his business, he'd have given you ten lashes on the spot!"

I was so unwise as to answer that I could not be blamed for doing my master's bidding.

"Don't talk to me, don't talk to me, you infernal scoundrel! I'll teach both you and your master what it is to insult a gentleman! Lay hold of him, Matt!"

Between the two of them they got me down, stripped off my coat, and bound my feet. Then Captain Robinson, before remounting his horse, beat me with his whip until it broke. A light riding whip cannot inflict the pain, or in any way make a proper substitute for the cowhide.

The Captain rode off, followed by Matt. I let them get well off, before untying my ankles. I looked about for my coat and hat, but they had disappeared. Matt's temptation to appropriate these articles was understandable. He would never be issued such good clothing at the Robinson plantation. Still, their theft added more coals to my anger at the treatment I had just received.

I reported at once to Major Thornton. When his fury had cooled somewhat, he remarked that the county court was to meet next day, that he would go to town, consult his lawyer, and make sure that this time the full force of the law would be brought against the man who had the effrontery to abuse and despoil *his property*.

I was taken along to the lawyer's office next day and gave a full report of what had happened to me. Major Thornton then demanded that the lawyer set the wheels

74

in motion to bring Captain Robinson before the bar of justice. The lawyer answered that the law in this case was very clear.

"Some people," he said with every show of indignation, "will assert that the law in the slaveholding states does not protect against the violence of whites. They will say that any white man may flog any slave at his own good pleasure. Not true, sir! The law permits no such thing! If a slave is assaulted, the master of that slave (his legal guardian and protector, as you know, sir) can bring action for damages. In this case it is quite plain that you have good ground for action against Captain Robinson. All we need to do is bring forward proof of the facts of the case."

"We have the facts well in hand," said Colonel Thornton. "They are as the boy here stated."

"Yes, yes, to be sure," said the lawyer. "And what witnesses can you summon to back up these statements of his?"

"Why, the welts on his back are witness enough! His hat and coat have been purloined. A search will reveal them in the possession of one Matt, servant to Captain Robinson. There's your evidence of what went on."

"You seem to forget, Major Thornton, that the law requires we have a white witness to vouch for charges brought by a slave against a white man."

"Why, the devil take such a law!" the Major cried.

He carried on at such a great rate that I believe the lawyer was as concerned as I was that his rage would kill him. I was relieved when he turned and bolted out the door, shouting that he would have justice.

I hastily followed him into the street where he came

75

face to face with Captain Robinson, who had doubtless come to town to enjoy the crowds and conviviality surrounding county court day. My enraged master snatched at his pistol, blind to everything but getting his "justice." The two shot simultaneously. My master's shot was off the mark, but Captain Robinson's aim was true. When I bent over Major Thornton, he was already dead.

Such affrays are common enough in the South. The grand jury very seldom hears anything of them. And the conqueror is pretty sure to rise in the public estimation.

It is the lot of the slave, as of all other men, to be exposed to all the calamities of chance and caprices of fortune. But unlike other men he is denied the consolation of struggling against them, and his sufferings are aggravated tenfold by the bitter idea that he is not allowed to help himself or to make any attempt to escape the blow which threatens him. This feeling of utter helplessness is one of the most distressing in nature.

The alarm and terror which the news of Major Thornton's death excited at Oakland was very great. His slaves looked at each other in speechless consternation. They said little or nothing about the calamity, but the tears of the men and the cries and lamentations of the women were truly distressing. We all attended the funeral and followed our dead master to the grave. The thud of the earth on the coffin echoed in every heart. Doubt not the sincerity of our sorow. It was for ourselves we lamented.

An overseer and two assistants had appeared at Oakland on the very day of the tragedy, recruited and sent out posthaste by the lawyer. He himself shortly appeared and shut himself in the library, going over the master's papers. I was in constant attendance, serving his meals there, taking care of his wants, and meantime making preparations for his accommodation on the plantation and for the expected arrival of the Major's relatives.

Major Thornton had never married and had left no children. If he intended to make a will, his sudden death had prevented his doing so. His property passed to several cousins, for whom I suspect he did not entertain any great affection. He had not mentioned them within my hearing. It was thus that we became, with cruel suddenness, the property of strangers.

These heirs-at-law were as poor as they were numerous. They seemed very eager to turn the property into money and to get their several shares as soon as possible. I was on occasion excused from the study and posted outside the door while the gentlemen within discussed, as I thought, the sale of the plantation and all its human souls to a new master. The secret, which was very well kept and which I did not suspect, was that everything was to be sold piecemeal as quickly as possible, the slaves to be disposed of at once.

It was thought, I suppose, that if we got wind of the affair some of us would try to escape. This is doubtful. Armed guards patrolled the grounds. Our neighbors and their henchmen gratuitously patrolled the *public* roads with the intention of apprehending, even killing, any runaway *private* property of the late

Major Thornton. These neighbors, who had always said that a slave uprising in our part of the country would start with Major Thornton's "spoiled niggers," feared us most at the time of our greatest affliction and helplessness.

The day before the one which had been appointed for the sale, we were collected together. The able-bodied men and women were handcuffed and chained in a long line. A few old gray-headed people and the younger children were carried in a cart. The rest of us were driven along like cattle—men, women, and children together. Three fellows on horseback, with the usual pistols strapped on, and equipped with long whips, served as guards and drovers.

I shall not attempt to describe our afflictions. It would be but the repetition of an oft-told tale. Who has not heard of the slave traders on the coast of Africa? Our case was much the same. We knew the terror and despair of those kidnapped victims. Most pitiable were the wails of the women and the cries of the terrified children. The whips cracked, and the sorrowful procession was kept moving.

We lodged that night by the roadside, reaching the county courthouse the next day at the time appointed for the sale. The company gathered there was not large, since the notice of the sale had been so recently posted. The assembled bidders seemed extremely shy. Many of our neighbors were present, but no bids came from that quarter. We went off at very moderate prices. Most of the younger men and women and a large proportion of the children were bought by a slave trader who had come to bid from some distance, having been sent a special notice of the auction—for he had the reputation of being always on the lookout for "good stock." Some of the very old slaves could not be sold at all that day. I do not know what became of them.

Chapter 9

Our new owner was a slave-dealing firm whose headquarters were in the city of Washington, the seat of the Federal Government and the capital of the United States of America. The whole purchase was about forty head, consisting in nearly equal proportions of men, women, and children. The men were fastened in pairs by iron collars about their necks. A heavy chain was connected to links in these collars, the chain extending from one end of the drove to the other. In addition, the left and right hands of every couple were handcuffed together, and another chain passed along these fastenings. This extra bit of "reasonable security" was stated by our drover to be necessary because Thornton slaves were known to be "a set of very dangerous fellows." Women and older children were more lightly chained.

The drove was presently put in motion. The journey was slow, sad, and wearisome. I shall not dwell upon the monotony of it, nor on our sufferings. After several days we crossed the noble and wide-spreading Potomac and, late at night, began to enter the Federal city. The

Capitol reared spacious walls in the moonlight, a magnificent edifice. Lights gleamed from the windows. Perhaps Congress was in session.

I gazed at the building with no little emotion. Here was the headquarters of a great nation. Here was concentrated the wisdom to devise laws for the benefit of the whole community, the just and equal laws of a free people, a great democracy! These were ideas I had heard early in life from Colonel Moore and his friends.

But I now heard more clearly, close at hand, the clanking of chains and the cracking of drovers' whips. Here within a stone's throw of the very temple of liberty, the most brutal, odious, and detestable tyranny found none to rebuke or forbid it.

What sort of liberty is it whose chosen city can tolerate a slave market within its borders?

What sort of freedom is it that permits the bravado and insolence of a slave-trading aristocracy to lord it in the very halls of her legislature?

We passed up the street which led by the Capitol and presently arrived at the establishment of Savage, Brothers & Company, our new masters. Half an acre of ground, more or less, was enclosed with a wall some twelve feet high, armed at the top with iron spikes. In the center of the enclosure was a low brick building having a few narrow, grated windows and a stout door, well secured with bars and padlocks.

In common with all the slave-trading gentry, Messrs. Savage, Brothers & Company had the free use of the city prison. But they traded on so large a scale that the public jail could not accommodate all their property, and so they had been obliged to build this prison of their own. It was under the management of a regular jailer and was very much like any other jail. Slaves were allowed the liberty of the yard during the daytime but at sunset were locked up promiscuously in the prison. This was small and ill ventilated, and the number of human beings packed into it was sometimes very great. While I was confined there, the heat and stench were often intolerable. Many a morning I came out of it with a burning thirst and a high fever. I was, in addition, very filthy and an offense to myself.

The District of Columbia, which includes the city of Washington, is situated between the states of Maryland and Virginia and has now become (from the convenience of its situation and other circumstances) the center of slave-trading operations. The District shares the honor, however, with Baltimore and Richmond, chief towns of the two states mentioned.

As is well known, the states of Maryland and Virginia claim the honor of having exerted themselves for the abolition of the African slave trade. It is true that they were in favor of that measure. They had good reasons of their own for being so. They gained credit for holding humane principles and, by the same vote, secured for themselves the monopoly of a domestic trade in slaves which today bids fair to rival any traffic ever prosecuted on the coast of Africa. The African traffic they have declared to be piracy, while their own flourishing domestic trade they have the effrontery to proclaim a just, legal, and honorable commerce!

The lands of Virginia and Maryland have been exhausted by the miserable and inefficient system of cultivation which invariably results where farms are large and laborers enslaved. Rare indeed is the plantation owner who knows or cares anything about true husbandry. Yet there are those who imagine that masters somehow are able to transmit knowledge and care they do not possess to the men they drive every day to exhausting toil in exhausted fields! And those others— those who expect husbandmen to spring up spontaneously among uneducated and degraded men, and demand that the poor wretches practice the precious art *for the sole benefit of another and none of their own* —do they not court unreason to the point of madness?

Maryland and Virginia, then, raise the same crops as do several of the free states to the north and west, but their slave-labor produce cannot profitably compete with the more abundant and better-quality produce from free-labor states. They cannot meet such competition. They sink under it. Many a Virginia planter can only bring his revenues even with his expenditures, or show a little profit, by selling a few slaves every year. This practice is jocularly but most significantly known as "eating a Negro"—a phrase worthy of a slaveholding humanity. It is becoming more and more common every day to "eat a Negro." The Southern market is as regularly supplied with slaves from Virginia as it is with mules and cattle from Kentucky.

But the slave trade in America, as in Africa, carries with it the curse of depopulation. It has (together with the emigration which is constantly going on) already unpeopled great tracts of country in the lower part of Virginia. The first seats of Anglo-American population are fast being returned to all their original wildness and solitude. Almost whole counties are grown up in useless

83

and impenetrable thickets, already retenanted with deer and other wild game, their original inhabitants. How long ago it seems that James and I, when about ten or twelve years of age, had seen this condition at the "haunted" plantation north of Spring Meadow, and shivered; perhaps for the wrong reason, but we were children.

But to return to the Savage, Brothers & Company jail. We were packed in among perhaps a hundred other human beings, most of whom we later discovered to be young men and women between the ages of eighteen and twenty-four, closely packed on the bare floor, half naked, extremely filthy.

A considerable number had started up at our entrance and now began to crowd about us in this eerie place which was lighted only by feeble moonlight that fell in pale rectangles into the gloom. The curious pressed close to inquire who we were and whence we came. But we were fatigued. We sank down in the spaces somehow made for us, and in spite of the confined and impure atmosphere, we were soon buried in profound slumber.

Sleep is the dearest solace of the wretched. And there is this sweet touch of mercy in it—that it ever closes the eyes of the oppressed more willingly than those of the oppressor. I hardly think that any member of the firm of Savage, Brothers & Company slept so soundly that night as did the most desolate of their newly purchased victims.

In the morning we were let out into the prison yard. A scanty allowance of corn bread was doled out to us

84

for breakfast, and thus began the first of ten days we spent in that accursed place.

The men slaves who were gathered there were more numerous than the women, although the females had received a considerable addition from our party. The acquaintance of these newly arrived young women was eagerly sought. They were constantly receiving solicitations to enter into temporary unions, to last while the parties remained together. Most of the females whom we found in prison had already made connections of this sort, but with the arrival of our young ladies additional courtships, if so they may be called, were begun.

People danced in this place, on the hard-packed ground. A fellow with a three-stringed violin struck up a tune, and soon, in the corner of the yard where he held forth, young men and women were dancing, shouting, and laughing. They became wonderfully boisterous as the fiddler, who was remarkably nimble with the bow, played faster and faster, and the dancers strove to keep time, stay with him, and outlast him.

Another interesting diversion was that provided by a preacher who, in another corner, struck up a Methodist psalm. The crowd about him increased, and soon other voices joined in the singing until at times the chorus drowned out the fiddler. After the singing, the preacher prayed. His hands clasped, eyes raised to heaven, he spoke with great feeling and earnestness. His congregation responded to his words with a litany of shouts and praises to the Lord.

The text of the exhortation that followed was from

Job on the well-known subject of patience. The preacher soon deserted his original topic and ran on from one thing to another. It was a strange farrago, with now and then some sparks of sense to be followed by a flood of absurdity. Still, it was delivered with such volubility, earnestness, and force that it produced a strong effect upon the hearers. Groans and cries of "mercy" and "amen" became louder and more frequent. In some of the congregation the contagion of this spiritual intoxication was so great that, overcome by their emotion, they fell to the ground in screaming or moaning paroxysms. I myself felt a strong impulse to rush into the crowd and scream and shout with the rest.

Yes, even we who were penned up in the Savage, Brothers & Company prison yard valued our wretched lives, and in the ways open to us we celebrated life and hope. In prison we were on holiday—for are not holidays blessed days of relief from toil? We made the best of our "holy days" of idleness.

In due course, Savage, Brothers & Company selected from their warehouse a cargo of about fifty slaves for the Charleston market, I among them, and loaded the lot aboard the brig *Two Sallys*. The vessel was the property of a rich and respectable merchant of Boston.

Before leaving the prison, we were handcuffed and, having reached the wharf, were crammed into the hold of the vessel so close together that we had room neither to lie nor to sit in comfort. Once or twice a day we were suffered to come on deck to breathe fresh air for a short time, then remanded back to our dungeon. On these occasions of liberty our eyes were filled with sights

86

never before beheld; scenes of the river shore, the great bay, the capes of the Chesapeake, and at last the expanse of gray water that was the mighty Atlantic.

We had been a day or two on the Atlantic, most of us suffering from the close confinement and from sea-sickness, when a furious gale came on. The tossing and pitching of the ship was terrible indeed to us poor prisoners confined in the dark hold and expecting at every boom of thunder that the vessel would split apart. The noise and tumult on deck, the creaking of the rigging, the cries of the seamen, and the cracking of spars and splitting of canvas added to our terror. The hatches were finally opened; we were allowed on deck; and our fetters were knocked off.

A dim and horrid glimmer, more terrible perhaps than total darkness, hovered over the ocean. In the distance huge black waves, crested with pale blue foam, bore down on us, threatening to engulf us. In one instant our battered ship was sunk into a trough walled by towering black precipices; in the next we were lifted to the top of a lofty wave, and our terror-stricken eyes saw all around a fearful waste of dark and stormy waters.

The vessel had sprung a leak and was in great danger of foundering. The more able-bodied among the slaves were sorely needed to man the pumps. We worked with a will, but the leak gained on us, and within the hour the captain determined to abandon ship. He, of course, did not notify his cargo of his intention. The longboat had been washed overboard, but the crew had succeeded in securing the jolly boat which was now

87

lowered away and dropped into the water under the vessel's lee. The crew was already debarking before we understood what was afoot.

We rushed frantically forward and demanded to be taken aboard. Three or four pistols were fired, wounding some of us. Others were injured by cutlasses in the hands of sailors. The crew demanded that we stand back, saying that we would be taken off when all was ready.

Terrified and confused, we backed away. In this interval, made eerie with lightning flashes and noisy with almost constant thunderclaps, the rest of the sailors jumped into the jolly boat. "Cast off!" shouted the captain. The seamen bent to their oars, and the boat had moved off before we realized that not one of us, not even the women and children, would be accorded space although the boat was not full. Three or four slaves leaped into the water with the insane idea of reaching the boat and being saved. All but one sank immediately. That one landed close to the boat and managed to grasp the rudder. He was shot in the head. He let go his hold and disappeared.

Chapter 10

Some of our women screamed frantic supplications to their God; others clutched children to them in wordless terror; still others, weeping and praying, tended our wounded and tried to stanch their wounds with strips torn from their clothing. Spray dashed over us continually, and every few minutes we shipped a sea which set the decks awash and drenched us in salt water.

I and some of the other men found ourselves again at the pumps. Was this not supreme idiocy, since the captain himself had realized the futility of trying to keep afloat a vessel that took in more water than could be pumped out? But there we were, shouting, "Pump, my hearties! Pump for your lives!" This was the phrase the captain had used constantly as he stood over us, directing our labors. Perhaps we thought the pumps could not work without this incantation. We kept on until one of the pumps broke, and, shortly afterward, another became choked and useless.

Exhausted and almost spent, we looked about us. The storm had abated, and the vessel, though it rolled

89

drunkenly in the long swells and listed at a most dangerous angle, was still afloat. Presently the clouds began to break away and to drive in large and misty masses along the sky. A scene that remains in my mind is of a woman cradling her dead husband in her arms. He had been mortally wounded by one of the pistol shots. So fierce and dumb was her shock and grief that no one, for the present, dared to go near her to try to comfort or reason with her.

Some of us went below and overhauled the steward's supplies, all more or less damaged by salt water. We found a case or two of bread which was edible and doled out small amounts to our passengers.

Within two hours we discovered a vessel standing toward us. Having run down pretty near, she hove to and sent a boat to us. It was not long before the visitors mounted over the brig's side. They seemed almost stunned at the scene we presented.

The mate of the vessel approached me and asked where the rest of the crew was. I explained that we were a cargo of slaves, that the crew had deserted.

"All except you," he growled. He seemed displeased that any crew member remained on board. I told him that I was not a sailor but a slave. He glowered and seemed doubtful. I turned, perhaps with the idea of enlisting my companions in support of my statement, and as I did so, one of the visitors said, "Blimey, he's a slave, all right. Look at his back."

"Must be," said the mate. "Never saw such a white one before. All right, you!" he said, addressing me. "I'll report to my captain, and we'll be back. Keep order here."

90

"Yes, sir," I answered.

The quiet that had prevailed during this exchange was uncanny. Even the whimpering of the children was subdued. When the mate and his party had gone over the side, some of us found our voices. There were exclamations of praise to the Lord that we had come through and were to be saved. Questions were addressed to me. I confronted a perfect sea of dark, imploring eyes. What did they expect of me? The ways of the sea were as strange to me as to any of them. I had no idea what was to become of us.

I caught the glance of one of the stout fellows who had worked at the pumps. His gaze seemed to be especially keen and probing.

"Well, Jeff?" I asked.

"There's time to eat before they get back," he said.

Some of us dashed below and hauled up every edible morsel of bread we could find. We had the good fortune to come upon an undamaged cask of fresh water and ladled it out.

Soon carpenters and mechanics from the other ship came aboard, got the pumps in order, and set us to working them, while they made makeshift repairs on the masts and sails. At length we got underway with a strange skeleton crew, so ignorant of slave management that they neglected to push us into the hold. Before night we made land, and a pilot came on board. The next morning we anchored in the harbor of Norfolk. We were shackled, hurried off the *Two Sallys*, and locked up in the Norfolk city jail.

We were in a subdued and melancholy frame of mind, for we had buried our dead passenger at sea. Psalms

91

sung for him, and for those of our company who had perished when they leaped into the sea, lingered in our minds long after the singing had ceased. True, it happened that none among us was a preacher; but among slaves almost anyone can step forward and conduct a burial if need arises, for the lowliest among us have become familiar with the procedure through frequent attendance at these sad ceremonies.

We remained in this jail for three weeks, not knowing why we were kept there or what was to become of us. What had happened was that our rescuer, the *Arethusa* out of New York, had claimed the *Two Sallys* and her cargo for salvage. We were to be held until we could be sold at auction. This was the final disposition of the Savage, Brothers & Company's cargo, originally destined for disposal in the Charleston market.

We had sailed for Charleston in a Boston-owned ship, had been salvaged by a New York-owned vessel. Yet people of the Northern states talk grandly on the subject of slavery and express a very proper indignation at its horrors!

Recall, if you will, that while the African slave trade was permitted, the merchants of Northern free states profited from it; and now these same merchants do not always refuse to employ their vessels in the domestic slave trade.

Is the domestic trade one iota less base and detestable than the African?

Consider the facts concerning these grand-talking men—statesmen, lawyers, judges—of the free North. They have permitted slavery to exist where it need not exist, for nothing in the Constitution makes slavery mandatory anywhere in the United States of America. Through the instrument of a Federal law enacted in 1793, they have allowed the Constitution to be defamed and defiled by making it obligatory for Northerners to catch, hold, even kill escaped slaves, in their zeal to restore them to their Southern owners. And they demand that the letter of this fugitive slave law must be scrupulously observed everywhere among the citizenry and at all levels of government.

Yet what of the laws of the nation and the laws of humanity—laws older and more sacred than this fugitive slave law? What of our precious laws protecting against unjust imprisonment, against torture and murder? *Free* American citizens, black and white, suffer and die in the South every day under the most blatant abuses of our basic democratic statutes. From the lips of grand-talking Northerners comes no demand that these laws of our democracy be scrupulously observed in the South, to equal their demand and insistence that slavery's law be observed in the North!

These Northern aristocrats, in the energy of their hatred for slaves and for free men of any complexion who would speak and act for the slave, reveal a positive envy of the Southern aristocrat. A man who can return an escaped slave to his master has a deep sympathy with the master and little difficulty in imagining himself a member of the master class. He is a positive enemy of democracy. He does not love democracy or equality. His love lies elsewhere.

The Northern states of the Union dare assert that they are undefiled by the stain of slavery! They boast in vain. They are partners in the wrong. The blood of slavery is

93

on their hands and drips from the hems of their garments.

I had already been twice sold at public auction, the thing had lost its interest and novelty for me, and I found my third auction much like other slave sales.

Jeff and I and two other young males were purchased by an agent of Mr. James Carleton of Carleton Hall; the plantation was located in one of the northern counties of North Carolina, and presently we set off for our new home. We were in charge of the agent and two drovers of his, who kept sharp watch around the clock, during the four days and nights of our journey. We were prime young bucks, and no doubt our guards thought us very dangerous. In reality we may have never in our lives been less dangerous. We had just escaped a watery grave and, if I may judge the others by myself, felt something like gratitude to be treading God's good earth in the open air, even while dragging chains, and to have the starry sky overhead when we lay down at night. Every slave dreads going farther south, and this circumstance depressed us, but I do not believe any of us entertained thoughts of escape.

I always looked for the North Star before closing my eyes, for north lay Virginia and Cassy. Because she was closer to that bright star than I, I sometimes imagined her free. I did not long for her so much as for her well-being and happiness. And even while walking steadily away from Virginia, I had every intention and hope of making my way back to Spring Meadow and of seeing my beloved wife again.

During the march I had much time to speculate about this Carleton Hall we were destined for, and had come to the conclusion that a plantation known by so fine a name must have something grand and baronial about it. If one must be a slave, thought I, better be a slave at Carleton Hall than at some of the miserable plantations we passed on our journey.

But Carleton Hall, despite its pretentious name, was as mean a place as any we had seen on the way. The "hall" was a large wooden house of haphazard design. Three generations of Carletons had evidently added rooms and annexes as families grew and space was needed. The whole was in a sad, if not scandalous, state of disrepair. There were no signs of ornament or comfort anywhere about the place. Slaves lived in a miserable collection of ruinous cabins, almost concealed in a vigorous growth of weeds and brush.

We were turned into one of the hovels, and a guard was posted outside. After sundown, and when we had decided that we had been forgotten, the door opened. The aperture was almost closed again by the huge frame of the black man who stood there. He informed us to come out, as our supper had arrived.

This man was Thomas, an African of unmixed blood; his complexion a glossy ebony, his features strong and good, he was a man of unusual stature and muscular frame, and a very remarkable individual on several accounts. In time I was to learn that he had been orphaned when very young, his parents having been slaves of a Methodist planter. This man had evidently considered his first duty a scrupulous care for the souls of his charges. When Thomas was sold away at age fifteen, he not only believed but he lived by the Christian precepts he had learned. He believed that God

95

had made him a servant and that it was his duty to obey his master and be contented with his lot. If his master smote him on one cheek, he was to turn to him the other also. With Thomas this was not a mere form of words run through with and then forgotten. In all my experience I have never known a man over whom his creed appeared to hold so powerful a control.

While the guard lolled, nodding, against a tree, Thomas stayed on talking with us. It was going on toward midnight before we went back into the hovel. This man's visit had served to quiet our apprehensions about what lay in store for us. He was only a slave but, on his own initiative, had made us welcome to the miserable place—which became, as a consequence, less miserable in our eyes and allowed us to feel that perhaps our fortunes had taken a turn for the better.

The next day, having been issued clothing that was not new but at least clean, we were ushered into Mr. James Carleton's study to be presented to our new master. My first impression here was one of astonishment, as the room seemed to be walled not with walls but with books!

The lamented Major Thornton had had a goodly shelf of books, mostly on agricultural subjects, and a great part of his collection I had read—not always with complete comprehension but always with interest and a feeling that comprehension would increase in proportion to the desire for knowledge. But let us have done with these books of Mr. James Carleton's. There were 345 of them, by my actual count, mostly on theological subjects but many of a general nature. While I lived there, I never sat down to read one of them from cover to

96

cover, but read in snatches while leaning against the shelves, a Bible in my hand. Anyone entering the room invariably found me leafing through the Bible.

The agent put me forward as a trained house servant. But so excited was I at the sight of the books, and of the pamphlets and newspapers scattered about on tables and the floor, and of Mr. Carleton's desk awash with sheets of foolscap—evidence that our visit had interrupted the master in an important bit of writing—that I made bold to speak. I said, humbly but firmly, that I could read and write.

Mr. Carleton was startled and, alas, disagreeably so. He snorted, drummed impatiently on the desk with his fingers, then turned to the agent and said, "We will try him in the house. If he doesn't work out, Mr. Warner can always use another hand in the fields."

Once again my arrogance or my sense of my own worth had almost betrayed my own best interests. For a month I believe I said nothing but "Yes, sir" or "No, sir," never speaking unless spoken to.

I served Mr. Carleton so assiduously, anticipating his every wish, and smoothing the way for the overworked and harried Mrs. Carleton at mealtimes, that I made myself seemingly indispensable. "Whatever did we do before Archy came?" that good lady would sometimes say, but never within Mr. Carleton's hearing.

There were six Carleton children—the oldest a girl of thirteen, the youngest a mere infant. I was able to settle many disputes among them, and I must say that my association with these children is one of the pleasant memories of my stay at Carleton Hall. I suppose these young ones reminded me of my young master and

97

brother, James, and the childhood pleasures we had shared.

The truth is that I benefited, as house servants often do, from the fact that some men (but more especially women and children) cannot have any living thing about them—be it a dog, a cat, or even a slave—without insensibly contracting some interest in it and some regard for it. Thus it is that a black house servant can often become quite a favorite and may at last be regarded with a feeling that bears some faint and distant resemblance to family affection. It is by steadily fixing their eyes on a few cases of this sort, and as steadily closing them to all the intrinsic horrors and enormities of slavery, that some bold sophists have mustered the courage to eulogize "the peculiar institution" of slavery!

Chapter 11

There are probably very few people in the world who when they are intimately known, prove to be genuinely simple souls; and of all people, the slaveholder is probably the least likely to be an easily understood person.

How shall I describe Mr. Carleton? He constantly presented in conversation and conduct an incongruous mixture of bully and Puritan. I use the word "bully" for want of a better—not exactly in its most vulgar sense but to suggest a certain spirit of bravado and violence. He was as ready as any other Southerner to settle a dispute with a pistol. Yet he was a pious man, an evangelist, a passionate lover of the Bible, and strict and Puritanical in his insistence that all people live "according to the Word."

In this man there seemed to be, at one and the same time, a secret consciousness of criminality and a fixed determination never to admit it. At the slightest suggestion from any quarter that there was anything wrong about the care, feeding, or treatment of slaves (his own or another's), he would launch blindly into an intemperate declamation against impertinent interference in the affairs of other people. This harangue is all too commonly indulged in by those whose own *affairs* will hardly bear close examination.

Now this man knew less about his own affairs than I did after living with him for half a year. I make bold to say that only one other person on the place knew more of Mr. Carleton's affairs than I did, and that person was Mr. Warner, the overseer.

Mr. Warner was shrewd, plausible, intelligent, and well acquainted with his business. I say "his" business advisedly, for Carleton Hall was run in the interest of Mr. Warner, not of Mr. Carleton. Mr. Warner was engaged on terms which, however ruinous to the planter and his plantation, were very common in Virginia and the Carolinas. Instead of receiving a regular salary, he took a certain proportion of the crop. It was in his interest to make the largest crop possible without any regard whatever for the means used in making it.

Mr. Carleton gave generous allowances of corn and meat to his slaves. He was widely praised for his liberality, especially concerning the meat, for most of his neighbors were not liberal at all with that article. But Mr. Carleton put the distribution of provisions into the hands of Mr. Warner. It was to Mr. Warner's interest to distribute just enough to keep the slaves alive and to distribute the balance elsewhere for his own profit. Our slaves were ill fed.

Thomas was so well trusted that on occasion Mr. Warner gave him the keys to the storehouses and the responsibility for distributing the allowances. These two differed in their estimates of what constituted a peck of dried corn. Mr. Warner had a careless hand and eye, and he would impatiently scoop out a portion, his understanding evidently being that a level measure was one with a depression in it. Thomas' understanding was that a true measure was one so rounded that great care must be used to move it from the barrel to the sack held eagerly forward by the slave.

Mr. Warner was given complete management (meaning discipline) of the slaves. Mr. Carleton's instructions to his overseer were to "get the work out of them." The master considered Mr. Warner a good and valuable overseer because the work got done somehow, the crops (such as they were) were got in, and no trouble was allowed to arise among the slaves, at least none that he need bother about.

As for land management, let us admit at once that in three generations of Carletons at Carleton Hall, it is possible that the land had never been cultivated with any tolerable skill. But under Mr. Warner the process of exhaustion had been carried to its last extremity. Field after field had been "turned out" as they call it. They were left uncultivated and unfenced, to grow up with broom sedge and persimmon bushes, and to be grazed by all the cattle of the neighborhood. Year after year new land had been opened and exposed to the same exhausting process, until at last there was little land capable of making a crop—let alone a good one. Mr. Warner hinted darkly that he might have to seek a more remunerative place of employment. New concessions from Mr. Carleton persuaded him to remain.

Mr. Warner's management of his human work animals had, at the time of my arrival, resulted in a col-

101

lection of forty or fifty of the most discontented, sickly, recalcitrant, and inefficient slaves I had ever seen gathered together. There was scarcely a week when one, two, or three of them were not runaways, wandering in the woods. A concerted search was rarely made for them. In time they would creep near—driven by a need for food or human companionship, or both. It often happened that one of these runaways was seen returning home in company with Thomas (though not in his custody). Whether slaves got from Thomas the moral strength to face their punishment or simply believed that his protection afforded them a degree of safety from intemperate and excessive reprisal, I am unable to say.

Mr. Carleton had family prayers night and morning, behind a closed door. He prayed long and fervently on his bended knees, his wife and progeny on their knees about him. He was president of the state Bible Society and the burden of his prayer was an earnest petition for the universal spread of the Gospel. Yet at the very moment that he professed to prostrate himself in the dust before his Creator and proclaimed that all men were the creatures of the same God, he felt too strongly the sense of his own superiority to permit even his household blacks to participate in his devotions! In this he was, unbeknownst to himself, unsuccessful. Aunt Katy, the old nurse who had tended him since baby-hood, hovered near the door and followed to the letter the ritual within; and the other servants fell silent as they went about their light Sunday duties and in low voices joined in prayer and song.

Our master was not a clergyman. There were few

clergymen in that part of the country, so he had filled the need by becoming an exhorter. He assiduously tended the vineyards of the Lord, while neglecting his own. There was never a Sunday that he did not hold forth somewhere, and he was always sure of a pretty large audience. The religious flocked to him; but others also attended who were not so religious as they were glad of any occasion for assembling together, for there were but few amusements of any kind in that region.

In summer Mr. Carleton often preached in a shady grove or beside a stream; in winter, at his neighbors' homes or in his own. And although he did not conduct daily prayer meetings for his slaves, he was generous in issuing passes for them to attend his public performances. All exhorters are inspired by large audiences, and Mr. Carleton was no exception to this. Our slaves and those of our neighbors were, of course, glad for the relief from the eternal monotony of their lives which these meetings afforded.

When Mr. Carleton thought of it, he took notice of his black listeners. Sometimes, toward the end of his preaching, he suddenly dropped the phrase "dear brethren" with which he always addressed his white listeners. He raised his voice so as to be heard clearly by the large assemblage of blacks standing some distance to the rear, and informed "those whom God hath appointed to be servants" that their hope for salvation lay in patience, obedience, submission, and diligence in performing their tasks. On occasion he varied his sermon for slaves by delivering a harangue on the sinfulness of thievery, a sermon that never seemed to take hold among his own slaves; for at Carleton Hall was a set of the most persistent, clever, daring, and successful raiders and marauders in the whole countryside.

One day my master said, "So you claim to be able to *write*. Eh, Archy?"

"Yes, Master Carleton."

"We shall see. Copy this." He pushed toward me the beginning of one of his numerous writings for the Bible Society. I sat down, and being able to decipher it, I made a fair copy. He could not well disguise his surprise, but his praise was a grudging "It will do."

The truth of the matter is that I write a very fine hand. Why would I not? My early experience had been to make my letters as perfectly as I could, so that James would have a fair model to copy, and painstakingly to guide my brother in correcting his errors.

"You *cipher*, too, no doubt?"

"My young master wanted me to learn along with him, to keep him company at his lessons," I said. I felt that I could not claim this skill without an apologetic explanation being offered. He gave me a column of numbers to add, and I did so.

Gradually I became a kind of secretary to Mr. Carleton and did a good deal of copying for my master. Much of it entailed the entering of some of Mr. Warner's scribbled notations about plantation business in a poorly kept and, to me, mysterious set of bound ledgers. It was in studying these ledgers and trying to understand them that I began to have a faint notion of the deplorable condition of Mr. Carleton's affairs.

About one year previously he had been so badly in debt and so harassed by creditors that he had made a hasty loan from some Boston moneylenders. The sum had been sufficient to pay off his clamoring creditors. For it, he had given his slaves as collateral. The loan was drawn for one year only. The year was about up, and during these last months Mr. Carleton had been trying to arrange a long-term loan, which would pay off the moneylenders and cancel the mortgage on his slaves.

His whole ruined plantation was to be the collateral for the new loan. He requested that the loan be of ten years' duration, to be paid off from the yearly profits of a plantation that did not show profits!

He had not been successful in securing such a loan and became progressively more worried, pessimistic, and impatient. At his angriest, he would sometimes make sarcastic remarks about Mr. Warner, who was so inconsiderate as to allow management worries concerning Carleton Hall to be inflicted on its owner.

"He's not getting the work out of them!" he once exclaimed, meaning that Mr. Warner was too indulgent with the slaves.

I, however, had been more and more often recalling Major Thornton's clover culture and other land-management theories and practices. Although I would have agreed that the Carleton slaves were a shiftless and conniving lot (made so in part, in my opinion, by Mr. Warner's "management"), I was inclined to put the true blame for the troubles on poor land management. It was because my thoughts ran in that direction that I ventured to mention my former master to Mr. Carleton. I told of the fine condition of Major Thornton's fields, regularly rotated to clover, and their remarkable yields when put back into other crops.

Mr. Carleton's indignation turned him to stone. I think I was in danger of being summarily dismissed to Mr. Warner's tender ministrations in the fields.

"This Thornton, I believe," he finally said, spitting the words at me, "was a *farmer*—in *middle Virginia*?" I knew well the planter's scorn for the farmer, but I did not know the source of Mr. Carleton's scorn for middle Virginia, nor do I to this day. I was thankful when I was able to escape on an errand a few minutes later.

I had made the mistake of supposing that when Mr. Carleton spoke aloud, he was addressing me and expected a response. I could not seem to learn that to members of the master class the slave, though present in the flesh, is never present as a person; that members of the master class do not consider that a slave can think, or that if he sometimes can think, do not want to hear what he thinks. I could not seem to learn the rule that any speech addressed to the slave will usually be in the form of an order and is in no case an invitation to conversation and exchange of ideas.

But almost as galling as Mr. Carleton's soul-destroying way of putting me in my place was the necessity of damming back what I considered highly exciting and significant information that might enable Mr. Carleton to make a paying proposition of his ruined plantation. My youth—I was but twenty-three and a most rustic twenty-three at that—must be blamed for the deep despondency into which Mr. Carleton's rejection of my help had plunged me.

It was a foolish and useless bit of information I had wanted to impart, as I now see. It was too late for

106

clover culture (a matter of long-term planning) to save Mr. Carleton from ruin.

In my defense, however, I must cite my optimism that the new loan would be forthcoming, and time for starting clover culture would thus be gained. I had copied out numerous communications to prominent, prosperous, and influential members of the Bible Society in the North, imploring that they use their good offices with a certain reputable financial house in New York, and that they strongly recommend to these bankers that the loan to Mr. Carleton be granted forthwith. I fully expected the brothers in the society to fly to the aid of their zealous North Carolina president.

After the evening meal at the house had been cleared away, and without stopping at the kitchen for the food the cook would have prepared for me, I went at once to Thomas' cabin. There I poured out my anger and frustration to my friend, who heard me to the end and then asked me to join him and his wife, Ann, in their evening meal.

Ann was a very tall woman and exceedingly thin. She did not move or speak with the verve and force which is associated with good health. Still, though slow, she was a good and steady field hand and accomplished as much or more than stronger workers who put more time and energy into devising ways of avoiding the task than they did in falling to and getting it done. (My sympathy was with these latter rascals; I had early learned, with Billy, that a task well and quickly done was rewarded by assignment to another.)

Ann held her daughter, who was barely six months

old, on one arm while preparing our meal; and the child lay across her lap while we ate, to be the recipient of many a loving pat and soothing word. The infant was small, sickly, and fretful. Thomas had often given thanks to God for her, explaining that Ann had lost two children at birth and that he and his wife had prayed unceasingly that the third might live. Ann spent every hour with her child, except when she was in the field. Then, of necessity, she must leave the baby at the edge of the field and return to her only at nursing time.

The hour I spent that evening with Thomas and Ann had its usual effect upon me. I left these good people feeling strengthened for the next day and in some ways a better man.

Chapter 12

Very early on a Sunday a few weeks later, my master and I traveled a good fifteen miles to a campground where he and other revivalists were to speak. Mr. Warner had denied passes to our slaves. The distance was too great, the day's events too extended, he said, and for these reasons our people, who would be making the journey on foot, would be unable to return until sunup on the Monday and would be unfit for that day's work.

The site for the meeting was a pretty one, a gentle swell of ground over which were thinly scattered a number of ancient and wide-spreading oaks. On the highest place a rude platform had been erected. Below and partially surrounding it, a number of benches had been placed, to be occupied for the most part by the ladies and the elderly.

People were arriving on horseback and by wagon and carriage. Slaves, who as usual greatly outnumbered the whites, came on foot from all directions. My master dismounted, was heartily welcomed by his friends, and escorted up the hill. I remained behind to care for the horses and to loll about with the other slaves, for I need not report to Mr. Carleton until the speaking ended late in the afternoon. When in public with my master, I was the hostler, not the secretary or even the attentive body servant.

On this day I lolled in the shade of an oak with other slaves who, like myself, had no interest in the hymns, prayers, and exhortations of the meeting. I had long since renounced that silly prejudice and foolish pride which, at an earlier period in my life, had kept me aloof from my fellow slaves and had justly earned me their hatred and dislike. Experience had made me wiser. I no longer took sides with our oppressors by joining them in their false notion of their own natural superiority. That notion, founded only in the arrogant prejudice of conceited ignorance, has long since been discarded by the more liberal and enlightened of the country. But it is a notion which is still the orthodox creed of all America; and it is the principle—I might say the sole foundation—which sustains the iniquitous superstructure of American slavery.

There were two other revivalists, in addition to Mr. Carleton, holding forth that day, and the platform continuously presented a lively scene. By far the majority of the slaves pressed as close behind the white spectators as was seemly, joined in the songs and prayers, and turned rapt faces to the fiery orators. Our women were especially engaged in the proceedings, leaving only to tend the fires started up for cooking the noontime meal, or to retrieve wandering children or box the ears of

110

noisy and quarrelsome youngsters. Some of the black men were out of sight in a grove, passing a bottle from hand to hand.

At the dinner hour, one of my new-found friends invited me to share the meal the women from his plantation had prepared. I did so with pleasure. Then, after moving the Carleton horses to fresh grass and hobbling them under the trees—for the day had turned oppressively hot—I stretched out in the shade with the intention of sleeping away the most sultry hours.

Presently I was aware that a drunken gang was approaching, their coarse laughter preceding them. The scent of wood smoke and simmering kettles had no doubt penetrated the grove and lured them from their retreat. The speech of one of them, or perhaps the familiarity of a peculiar laugh, prompted me to push my hat back off my eyes and to rise on one elbow to scrutinize the group as it lurched by.

"Billy!"

I was on my feet, had him by the arm, and pulled him from his companions. "Where did you come from and what are you doing here?"

The naturally lazy tongue of my old Spring Meadow fieldmate had been made more so by the liquor, but I managed to learn from him that Colonel Moore had sold him and some others shortly after Stubbs had carried me off; and that Billy had recently been sold again and now lived with a Mr. Winston Slocum not five miles from the campground.

When I questioned him about Cassy—had all gone well with her at Spring Meadow, was she well treated and happy?—Billy said, "She ran off, Archy. She was gone before you left!"

He told how Cassy had been brutally whipped, then confined to "Miss Ritty's house." Miss Ritty (Henrietta) was a light-skinned slave who had been installed some years before in the neat little place where my mother had lived and died. It was from there that Cassy had broken out one night, cutting through the rude wooden slats that barred the one window in her prison room. She had got "clean away"—and it was obvious that she could not have done so without a confederate.

Miss Ritty had sworn that she had nothing to do with the scheme. A beating and a month's confinement on a diet of hoecake and water had not changed her story. And Billy said that the last he knew, Miss Ritty had been returned to the little house, had it nice and pretty there, all to herself. He let out a shout of laughter, inviting me to share in his glee that Ritty had outsmarted Colonel Moore, had got rid of her rival, and had kept her privileged and envied situation at Spring Meadow.

Could I believe this poor fool and a drunken one at that? I had to. In my anguish I cried, "Then you don't know what became of Cassy? Is it thought she got off entirely, got to the North?"

"I don't know." He pulled weakly against my grasp on his arm, said he was hungry, said he had to get his dinner. His bloodshot eyes turned evasively this way and that, looking everywhere but at me.

I led him to one of the campfires where a good woman, grumbling all the while about the evils of drink, gave him some food. I sat beside him while he ate, then

112

led him away, sat him down, and said, "You know something you're not telling me, Billy. I will know what you know if I have to beat it out of you. I will have the truth, Billy."

Slaves in general have little regard for the truth. In general, the whites who lord it over the blacks do not themselves have a regard for the truth. A slave who is closely questioned will cast about in his mind not for the truth but for the words that will be most acceptable to the questioner. He tells the "truth" the white man wants to hear. And why not? In that "truth" lies his reprieve and his—at least temporary—safety.

I was certain that Billy knew something he was fearful of telling me, because it might anger me and he would suffer the consequences of my anger. I tried to allay his fears and kept at him until I wore him down. What I learned was as follows:

Billy had seen Cassy on the occasion of his second sale. She had not remained free long after her escape. She had been apprehended by a suspicious small farmer, had been sold by him when he needed the cash she and her baby would bring.

Yes, Cassy *and her child,* named Archy—a mere infant—had been sold together. The baby was blue-eyed like his daddy, black-haired like his mama, Billy said. Thus I learned I had fathered a son—and a slave.

I sat through the afternoon beside a wretched man who lay sleeping off the effects of his debauch. Thomas was in my thoughts. He had often said that Cassy and I would be reunited "in God's own time," and I was filled with a conviction that the time was near. When

113

Billy awoke, his mind would have cleared; he would remember who had bought my small family, and nothing would prevent me from searching them out.

My vigil was for nothing. Billy did not know the name of the purchaser.

But surely on the Slocum plantation there were others who had been purchased at that sale? Billy said that was true. Very well, I would question them. They might have been more observant than poor Billy. I determined to request a day's pass to go to the Slocum plantation, to see old friends there. Mr. Carleton would not refuse the request. For many months I had served him well and had earned one day's freedom for the pursuit of my own interests and pleasures.

When the meeting was over, Mr. Carleton showed the effects of the exertions of the day and of the heat. His face was flushed and glistening with sweat as he took a hasty farewell of the friends and sycophants who crowded about him. He gave as the excuse for his immediate departure, his fatigue and the distance he must travel.

We had gone but a short way when he called back to me, "Go on ahead, Archy. Prepare Mrs. Carleton and say that I'll want my supper set out."

"I'll need a pass, Master," I reminded him, as I drew alongside. "I may be stopped and questioned."

He impatiently scribbled the pass and thrust it toward me. I raced my horse in spurts and made the distance in good time. The reader will understand that my mind was not occupied with puzzling over why I should be sent ahead on a senseless errand. My master knew as well as I did that the women at Carleton Hall only

114

awaited the sound of the horse's hoofs in the carriage-way to lay out Mr. Carleton's supper. Delay in this matter was unimaginable.

No—my excited mind was occupied with thoughts of Cassy and of our child. Billy's news had, of course, been world-shaking for me.

I cantered onto the grounds at Carleton Hall, pulled up at the back of the house, and hastily dismounted. I would deliver the needless message before walking the animal to the stable. A stranger emerged from the back door. Another appeared at the corner of the house and strode toward me. Belatedly I was struck by the peculiar silence and loneliness of the place. Not a slave was in sight.

"You're Archy?" asked the stranger, coming up.

"Yes, sir."

"Secure him, Mr. Duncan." This to the second man who had come up.

"What is this?" I asked.

A quick glance around showed me Mr. Warner trotting toward us from the large barn. "Damn all, Archy, don't you cause no trouble!" he yelled, breaking into a run. The two near me grabbed my arms and had my wrists crossed and lashed together before I rightly knew what was happening.

Mr. Warner, coming up, ordered, "To the barn, Archy, march!"

"Move, nigger!" This from the man addressed as Duncan. He turned me roughly about, gave me a shove, and the three of them crowded close about me, prodding me onward. Stupefied as I was, I realized that there was but one explanation for what was transpiring at Carleton

115

Hall. The Carleton slaves had changed hands and now were the property of a faceless Mr. Boston Moneylender, whose agents were rounding up collateral for an unpaid debt and holding it in the barn.

I was pushed in, and the door was slammed and bolted behind me. The interior was dim, and heavy with the odor of hay and of fear. Some sixty souls were confined there, from the smallest baby to the oldest among them, old Aunt Katy.

I made out Thomas moving toward me in the gloom.

"Thomas! I had a horse under me. I had a pass. I was free. I could have got clean away!"

My friend rested his bound hands on my shoulder. My awful distress was mirrored in his face. He said with deep feeling, "It may be, Archy. God only knows."

"Only God knows," I groaned. "I'll never know. I lost my chance—"

I suffered the most bitter regret. It is from that time that I mark a change in myself that can perhaps be illustrated in this way: Had I a master today who found it necessary to post a reward for my capture, it would not occur to him to set down as an identifying characteristic, as my father had done: *Smiles when spoken to.*

116

Chapter 13

We were held for twenty-four hours while Mr. Carleton raced about the countryside, trying to raise the money with which to purchase some of us from his creditors. He succeeded in wheedling a few of his neighbors into buying his old nurse, two of her children and her grandchildren—in all, three adults and five young persons. These eight would remain with Mr. Carleton at Carleton Hall to make his bed, cook his meals, care for his children and his four-footed animals, and tend his kitchen garden. Mr. Carleton's promise and intention was to buy them back from his neighbors when his "affairs" were straightened out. Late in the afternoon of the second day, old Aunt Katy and her kin were removed from among us, after which Mr. Carleton came to pay us a farewell visit and condole with us in our misfortune.

He bade a sorrowful farewell to Thomas and Ann and some of the others who had been at Carleton Hall for many years, had caused no deliberate trouble, and for whom it may well be he had developed a sincere affection. I believe he experienced an equally sincere feeling of positive relief to be getting rid of a not inconsiderable number of lazy and unprincipled rascals who had caused his overseer endless vexation.

When Mr. Carleton's gaze happened to slide in my direction, he always found my eyes fixed on him and looked quickly away. He did not address me or come near me. The man gave every appearance of furtive guilt in regard to me.

Perhaps I was a conundrum to him. The *logic* of his peculiar, Christian-slaveholder way of thinking persuaded him I was his equal because I was white in color and a Christian; but the illogic of his feeling about blackness convinced him that a strain of black inheritance rendered me in fact black, incapable of true Christianity, and fundamentally and unalterably unequal and inferior. Here was a conundrum of his own devising that he could by no means solve. He would be happy to see the last of me.

He did not stay among us long. He left abruptly in a state of confusion and anger. The many of us who had listened attentively to his unwelcome condolences, looking at him fixedly all the while, were guilty of outrageous impertinence. That we displayed no sign of sorrow at the prospect of being torn from the miserable Carleton Hall, our master would attribute in impotent fury to the innate perversity and ingratitude of the slave. His anger and confusion were justified, for we were undeniably ungrateful for all our former "protector" had done for us "for our own good."

At dawn we were put into traveling order. A wagon carried provisions and the younger children. The rest of us were chained together in the usual fashion.

118

We were given unusually humane treatment by our new owners. On the third day the chains were taken off all except the least trustworthy—the young males. The caravan was on the road for the best part of three weeks and traveled many a weary mile, yet we were to arrive at our destination in better spirits and in better physical condition than was the case at the start of the journey. Our daily stint of travel stopped long before sunset. We built our fires and prepared our meals from the generous stores of provisions supplied by the drovers.

It was soon apparent that we were being fattened for the market and being put in a condition to bring the highest prices. This did not prevent us from wolfing down our hominy and returning to the fire for more. We relished the abundant food and the long, restful nights, and were happy for our good fortune, whatever the reason for it.

My regret at the missed chance for freedom, and the vanished opportunity to learn more about the whereabouts of my wife and son, did not leave me. The torture of furious and impotent emotions at first threatened to overpower me. But this settled into a dull and fixed misery which, once experienced, is not unlike the guilty man's remorse, too deeply rooted ever to be eradicated.

Ann walked beside Thomas whenever she could. Our bound hands did not prevent Thomas and me from taking turns in relieving her of the burden of the baby. The mite of humanity weighed next to nothing. When I raised my bound hands before me, the crook of my elbows provided a cradle. The baby slept always with a frown knitting her tiny brows and with her fingers, mere twigs, curled into weak fists. If I saw her often through a prism of tears, I make no apology for that.

We at length arrived at Charleston, the capital of South Carolina. We were allowed several days of idleness in a compound. During this time we were liberally fed, given new clothes, and were measured for shoes—even the children.

One day the head drover came and collected Jeff (the same who had been with me on the *Two Sallys*), another stout young fellow, and myself. We were taken out and placed under guards who were new to us. Thomas and his family soon joined us. Eventually two more field hands and their wives—who were also field hands—were added to the party. When we were assembled (the six males chained in a line) our head drover informed us that we had been purchased by a General Wilburforce and were on the way to one of his plantations, called Loosahachee.

We had surmised that we were to be taken to the Charleston market and were surprised at this turn of events. The explanation seemed to be that General Wilburforce was a regular customer of the Boston moneylender who had acquired us, and that the General trusted the agent to select from the ever new and changing "collateral" stock the "items" best suited to fill the General's "standing order." We had been saved the agony of the turning, pinching, and pounding of the auction block, to say nothing of the humiliating and degrading remarks of the would-be buyers. I say "would-be buyers" knowing full well what I say. Folks without a shilling in their pockets, unable to buy so much as a stewing hen, would shout their estimates of our worth from the sidelines, or swagger up on the platform and feel our flesh and judge its worth—as if they had the wherewithal to pay for it, low as their estimates were!

I was grateful to miss the slave auction. Thomas, however, gave no thought to this. He felt most keenly the abrupt severance, the cruel circumstance of being taken out of the compound and abruptly separated from his Carleton Hall friends, and this without warning and without an opportunity for leave-taking. I did not share his feeling and, in trying to understand it, learned something new about Thomas. He was a family man certainly, as the term is generally understood; but he was a family man in a wider application of the term. His family feeling was broad and deep enough to encompass all God's children. This man loved the Carleton Hall people, even the most rascally and troublesome among them, and perhaps most particularly these.

"It is God's will," he said. Yet he was sad and silent on the long day's march to Loosahachee.

I was eventually to become intimately acquainted with a part of lower South Carolina that must be one of the most barren, miserable, uninviting tracts of land in the universe. It is called, in the expressive phrase of the country, the Pine Barrens.

The Pine Barrens stretches from the Atlantic inward for eighty or a hundred miles. For a great distance the land is almost perfectly level and raised but a few feet above the surface of the sea. In general the soil is nothing but a thirsty sand which is covered for miles and miles with forests of the long-leaved pine. The tall, straight, and branchless trunks of the scattered pines rise like slender columns and are crowned with tufts of gnarly limbs. Through their long, bristly leaves the breezes murmur with a monotonous sound, much like that of falling waters or of waves breaking on a beach. The forest floor is matted either with the saw palmetto (a low evergreen), or it is covered with a coarse and scattered grass where herds of half-wild cattle feed in summer and starve in winter.

The trunks of the pines scarcely interrupt a prospect whose tedious sameness is broken only by tracts of almost impenetrable swamp. These are thickly grown up with water oaks, cypresses, bays, and other large trees. From their spreading branches and whitened trunks, long dusky moss hangs to the ground in melancholy festoons, the very drapery of disease and death. The rivers, wide and shallow, swell during spring and winter rains and frequently overflow their marshy banks, helping to increase the extent of noisome swampland.

Even where the country begins to rise into hills, it preserves its sterile character for a long distance. It becomes a collection of sandy hillocks thrown together in the strangest confusion. In many places not even the pine will grow. It gives way to stunted bushes of the dwarf oak. In other places the dwarf oak fails to find anchorage and the bare sand is drifted into dunes by the wind.

A great part of this barren country might be brought into profitable cultivation by the enterprising spirit of free labor. At present there are only some small tracts along the watercourses which have been found capable of improvement by the costly and thriftless system of slave labor.

The above description does not apply to the part of southern South Carolina lying along the seashore from the mouth of the Santee to that of the Savannah and extending, in some places, twenty or thirty miles up-country. The coast between the Santee and the Savannah is a series of islands—the famous Sea Islands of the cotton markets. The cotton produced on the higher and drier lands of the area excels in the length of its fiber and closely rivals silk in strength and softness.

The islands once supported a magnificent stand of evergreen oaks. The soil, though light, is remarkably fertile. In some cases it yields fortunes in cotton; in others—where fields can most easily be protected by embankments from tides and floods, where they can be divided and drained by dikes and ditches, and can most conveniently be irrigated by fresh water—treasures of rice are harvested.

What beautiful vistas these districts present! As far as the eye can reach, the scene is one of smooth, level, highly cultivated country, penetrated in every direction by creeks and rivers. The residences of the planters are often handsome buildings, placed on some fine swell to catch the most vagrant breeze, and shaded by a choice variety of trees and shrubbery.

These mansions are occupied by their owners for only a short time in winter. The lords and ladies are driven away by the listless and monotonous existence that is experienced by cultivated whites who are set adrift on a sea of uncultivated and debased blacks. They are driven away, too, by the humid, enervating, and unhealthy climate, which is much aggravated by rice cultivation. For the greater part of the year, this "absentee aristocracy" congregates in Charleston, or dazzles the cities and watering places of the North by an ostentatious show of profligate extravagance and reckless dissipation.

Slaves in the Sea Islands are ten times as numerous as the free population. Yet the whole of this rich and beautiful country is devoted to the support of a few hundred absent families, whose lordly, luxurious, and dissipated indolence renders them useless to the world and a burden to themselves.

And to make possible this mode of life for these few, more than a hundred thousand human beings are sunk into the very lowest depths of degradation and misery.

Chapter 14

General Wilburforce must be numbered among the grandest of the South Carolina grandees. Loosahachee was but one of five plantations he owned. We found it to be an extensive place. The able-bodied working hands numbered more than two hundred. Children, the elderly, house servants, stablemen, mill hands, mechanics, and the like, easily doubled that number. The other Wilburforce plantations were, I believe, equally extensive, equally profitable, and operated with a like precision.

I was ignorant of the South Carolina etiquette which requires from every slave an obsequious bearing toward every free man, a custom seldom expected in Virginia. I found that South Carolina etiquette expects the doffing of caps and bowing of heads to all "gentlemen" encountered in the ordinary way of travel. The need to step into the ditch and show proper deference and respect to any and all members of the master race must, without question, be galling to slaves. Of course, the poor wretches are bowing much of the time to men who do not own them or any *body* or any *thing* else.

But the slave is helpless. The law does not protect him from assault by any member of the white race who demands the deference due a white man of property, and this whether the particular individual is propertied or only hopes to be; it is enough that he is white, the color of the propertied. Thus, the law of a great democracy encourages the corrupt concept and law of slavery throughout the whole body of the citizenry, corrupting all. Is not the man who demands that another grovel before him as despicable and debased as the one who grovels?

We were taken to an annex of the big house, a wing of the grand edifice which served as the living quarters and office of the head overseer and manager, a Mr. LeFavre. His eyes, embedded in folds of ruddy flesh, were of such a washed-out gray that I supposed the almost total lack of color to be an indication of poor vision. Such was not the case. Mr. LeFavre was exceptionally keen of sight, in seeing what he looked for.

"Name?" he asked when it was my turn to step forward.

"Archy Moore."

"Archy Moore!" He lifted his pale orbs to my face. "And pray tell how long has it been the fashion among you fellows to have double names? Hereafter, you are *Archy*—and let that be the end of it." And with a stroke of his pen he eliminated half of me from his records.

I had taken the name of my master since leaving Spring Meadow, a not uncommon custom in Virginia and one thought harmless enough. But what went unremarked in my native state was considered damned impertinence in South Carolina. South Carolinians seem,

126

of all Americans, to have carried the theory and practice of tyranny to the highest perfection. They are jealous of everything that may seem in any respect to raise their slaves above the level of their dogs and horses.

"Yer a field hand," the man remarked.

"Yes, sir!" I said perhaps too quickly and eagerly, but I was taken by surprise. I had seen my name inscribed in Mr. Carleton's ledger as house servant. How had this been changed to field hand? Had Mr. Carleton, in going over his collateral with the moneylender's agent, declared me to be of no earthly use in the house but of perhaps some slight value in the field? He may have added, with his customary sarcasm, "The fellow fancies himself uncommon wise in the proper culture of crops!"

If the above conjecture hits near the mark, Mr. Carleton, while spitefully intending to humble and put me in my place, had unwittingly done me the greatest of favors. I had expected to be put to work in the house but had determined to get myself out of it, through stupidity, poor performance, and repeated acts of impertinence and insubordination.

Why should I choose the field to the house? In general, are not those of us who are house servants infinitely better off than those who are employed in field labor?

House servants are better fed and better clothed, and their work is much lighter. They are sure of the crumbs that fall from the master's table. And as the master's eyes and those of his guests would be offended by a display of dirt and rags in the dining room, house servants are comfortably clothed. Also, since it is a matter of ostentation to have a house full of servants, the work becomes light when divided among so many.

127

Sufficient food, comfortable clothing, and light work are not to be despised. Yet the condition of a household servant is often almost too miserable for endurance. While there are occasionally kind masters and good-natured mistresses, it happens too often that the master is a capricious tyrant and the mistress a fretful scold. The poor servant is exposed every hour of his life to a course of harsh rebukes and peevish chidings which are always threatening to end in the torture of the lash and which, to a person of any spirit or sensibility, can be more annoying even than the lash itself.

In what amounted to thanksgiving, then (if not high good spirits) I, along with the others from Carleton Hall, went off to a cotton field in the care of the driver of our gang, Mr. Hugh Farmington.

Mr. LeFavre had established a rule against loitering. This meant that the slaves at Loosahachee were to "look alive" and proceed from place to place with un-natural alacrity. Something I had not before witnessed was the sight of slaves, myself among them, emerging from crowded, beehive quarters in the morning *on the run*. Those who did not look alive enough to suit Mr. Hugh Farmington felt the cut of the rawhide.

At the end of the day, work-worn though we were, we summoned the strength to return to our quarters at a brisk pace. Our drivers (themselves weary and perhaps hankering for the evening's mug of grog) did not so assiduously enforce the loitering rule at sunset. They did not so relentlessly flail us to our rest as was the case when we set forth to do our master's work.

Ann had been sickly since coming to Loosahachee, as indeed was often the case with slaves brought from the north and set to work in the pestiferous atmosphere which prevails wherever rice is cultivated on a large scale. It is not true that black men are peculiarly fitted to withstand an unwholesome and enervating climate and the agues and fevers associated with it. But it was futile for a sick slave to plead sickness. Drivers declared themselves to be sick of talk about sickness; it was all a sham, and they would be imposed upon no longer!

Ann was one among us (and doubtless there were others) who was ill equipped by nature with either the temperament or the physical attributes necessary to respond to this most ridiculous loitering rule. She was murdered because of this, and not as slaveholders would maintain because she shammed sickness, was sullen, defiant, unmanageable, and disruptive.

The baby, as I previously mentioned, was by custom left at the edge of the field, and by nature's law Ann must go to her at nursing time. The infant was left beneath a bush, a tree, or in the shade of a ragged garment hung between stakes. She was given into the care of a girl of eight or ten years. Little girls of this age make the finest of nursemaids, tender and attentive. At times an event transpiring a short distance away might attract childish curiosity, but on these occasions some voice was certain to call out, "If you don't mind that child, I'll come whop you!" and this was enough to send the little nursemaid scampering back to her duties.

On a day a few months after our arrival at Loosahachee, Ann had nursed the baby and was returning with her across the field to put her down nearer the rows we would be working that afternoon. The young nursemaid, freed of responsibility, ran through the field some distance ahead of Ann. When the youngster came skipping past our gang, I, without ceasing work, turned my head—perhaps to locate Ann and greet her. My glance showed that she was, indeed, walking our way. Behind her came Mr. LeFavre astride his horse. Ann evidently heard or sensed his approach, for she stepped across a few rows to give the horse clear passage. I bent to my work.

Ann's scream jerked me upright. Mr. LeFavre, standing in the stirrups, whirled the cowhide—and the woman's neck and arms were laced with streaming crimson ribbons of blood. After the first shock of the attack, Ann had dropped the baby. She fell across the mite of humanity, shielding it as best she could, and shrieking her alarm in strangled cries.

Thomas was on Mr. LeFavre before the rest of us could take in and believe what we saw. The big man leaped repeatedly, his hands reaching for Mr. LeFavre's flailing arm. "In God's name, what she DO?" the enraged Thomas cried.

The horse shied, backed, and wheeled; and because of this, Mr. LeFavre, although he had turned his attention from Ann to Thomas and attempted to lay the cowhide on the latter, failed more than once in the attempt. Thomas was a man of great natural strength which was now made supernatural by reason of strong passion and reckless disregard for his own safety. He repeatedly leaped and threw himself at horse and cursing rider, and he succeeded in tearing the whip from the overseer.

This most astonishing feat was accomplished by Thomas alone. Not one of us went to his aid. Most sure am I that nothing but the base and dastard spirit of a slave could have endured that scene of female torture

130

and distress and not rushed to aid the one who had gone to her rescue. Sober reflection persuades that had we rushed in, we would have died on the spot. Mr. LeFavre was armed.

The whip in his hand, Thomas spun about and staggered this way and that, trying to get around the plunging horse to go to the side of his wife. Mr. LeFavre, unable to control the animal, yelled between obscenities, "Seize him! Seize him!" The scattered drivers were already running toward him.

Mr. LeFavre managed to fumble his pistol out of his pocket. He scrambled down, almost falling from his horse (he was an obese and awkward man). He cocked the pistol and fired. The shot went wild. Thomas darted away, followed in his flight by repeated shots. He sprinted a zigzag course across the field, turning his head often to look behind him. What his fleeting glances may have shown him were slaves spotted about the field in gangs, some standing, some huddled or prone, but all immobilized in horror and terror. Or perhaps Thomas looked for and saw only Ann, bent in anguish over their child. He reached the edge of the field and disappeared into a thicket.

Mr. LeFavre ordered Mr. Hugh Farmington and another driver to seize Ann, drag her half fainting to a whipping post, tie her, and strip her to the waist. Mr. Farmington then delivered a number of lashes to complete the "correction" Ann's husband had so scandalously interrupted.

Mr. LeFavre, on horseback once again, shouted orders to the drivers. The bulk of the slaves were to be driven to their quarters. Other drivers were to round up some of us to accompany them into the woods and act as beaters to flush Thomas out of hiding.

As I started off with the search party, I saw that one of the women (undoubtedly without permission) had run from the crowd to the baby, picked her up, and was returning to the line of march with her. The woman's wailing left no doubt but that the baby was dead. The first snake of the whip around Ann's shoulders had lain open the flesh of the infant's back and shattered the fragile rib cage. It was impossible that the little one could have drawn breath after the first shock. Ann died that night. Neither her frail body nor her gentle spirit could withstand the insensate violence that had cut her down that shining, peaceful afternoon.

We did not find Thomas. We were brought in and sent to our quarters well before sundown. Armed men, strangers to us, were posted conspicuously about. We knew there were others invisibly lurking. The alarm had been sounded far and wide. Hate and fear were armed and posted at every crossroad and along the highway, patrolling woods and watercourses, standing sentinel at every locked and bolted plantation house, for miles in every direction.

I knew well what they were saying in the dining rooms of the big houses as the wine was passed around. A savage had reverted to his primitive nature, had attacked his overseer, *had snatched the whip from the man, and had run off with it!* Only God's providence had prevented the overseer from being lashed with his own whip in the hands of a crazed nigger! If the fellow were not taken, if such an atrocious act of insubordina-

132

tion were not most signally punished, it would be enough to corrupt and disorder the whole neighborhood.

"Things are coming to a pretty pass! The next thing we know, they will be cutting our throats!"

On occasion slaveholders make profoundly prophetic statements, not dreaming how truly they prophesy.

We had been at work but a short while next morning when an emissary from Mr. LeFavre summoned Jeff and me to his office. Two overseers from neighboring plantations were there. We were cursed and harshly questioned about Thomas' escape and possible hiding place. We were told that the fact that there was an escape plot at Loosahachee was well known and that it was equally well known that we and Thomas were deeply implicated. We were advised to lead our questioners at once to the renegade's place of concealment. I ventured to suggest that Thomas, unaccustomed to water and a poor swimmer at best, had probably drowned in some bayou, river, or canal, and that heavy rains would one day swell the watercourses and float his remains to view.

Jeff and I were, in turn, lashed to the whipping post and given twenty stripes on our "bare backs, well laid on" as the law explicitly states.

I have no inclination to disgust myself or the reader with further descriptions of the torment of which in America the whip is the active and continual instrument. Yet I dare not flinch, for it is necessary for those who may never have visited a Southern plantation to understand what goes on at most of those places every day of the year, and to realize what I mean when I say that

133

the rack was a superfluous invention and that the whip, by those skilled in the use of it, can be made to answer any purpose of torture.

Mr. Farmington, with earnest good will, had worn out his arm on Jeff and me. What then? Why, on an order from Mr. LeFavre, Mr. Farmington was seized by other drivers and strung up. Mr. LeFavre handed Mr. Farmington's whip to a man standing near and ordered that ten stripes be laid onto Mr. Farmington's white and quivering flesh. His crime? Laxity in regard to Ann's habitual loitering. Mr. Farmington was then given the choice of quitting the premises without collecting his pay or of accepting a lowly job devoid of authority. He chose the latter.

What did Mr. LeFavre see—he of the perpetually inflamed flesh and pale eyes—as he looked about at this final tableau?

He saw a mortified, demoted, disgraced Mr. Farmington, *for the whip had been taken out of his hand.*

He saw a person promoted to a place of power— presumably a place of honor, respect, and confidence —*because he now held the whip.*

What of justice and humanity can be expected under the governance of men who themselves are governed by such damnable and twisted values as these?

Our new driver was a black man. Of the twenty-five to thirty assistant overseers at Loosahachee, a half or more were appointed from among the slaves; for throughout that part of South Carolina, it is under the inspection of mostly black drivers that the cultivation of plantations is carried on.

South Carolina overseers seem not to encounter difficulty in locating slaves ready to tyrannize over and to betray their fellow slaves. For men of a certain temper, the rewards of the position are attractive. Black drivers, of course, receive no pay. But they are granted double allowances, and they are invested with the unlimited and absolute authority of the master himself. They have a thousand little spites to gratify and a thousand purposes of their own to accomplish. They are the absolute masters of everything which any of their gang may possess, including the persons of the women.

Of all men, these black drivers are most bitterly hated. The black driver who means to retain his superior position at all costs will faithfully copy the arrogance and insolence of his overseer and will as shockingly abuse his power. As he is always among his gang, the aggravating weight of his authority is so much the heavier. He is but one of themselves, and the slaves are naturally more impatient of his rule than if the same dominion were exercised by one belonging to what they have been taught to regard, and in fact do regard, as a superior race.

Every slave on the plantation was drawn to the evening burial service for Ann and her baby. It was an outpouring of grief, and it may be an outlet for terror, that perhaps could have been in no other way contained. In any event, no effort was made to dam the overflowing of strong emotion that filled hundreds of hearts to bursting.

On a beautiful slope at a goodly distance from habitations were the many ridges and mounds of the slave cemetery. Some of the graves had been there for many

135

years, and were sunken and weed-grown. It was midnight before all who had come to hear the preacher, to sing psalms, to pray, to mourn, to beseech God's mercy in the vocal way of the slave, and to wander weeping and wailing among the graves, had returned to the plantation.

I remained to keep vigil all night beside the grave, since Thomas could not. In mourning the death of my friend's wife and child, I mourned the death of my own. I knew them to be dead to me, buried in the great graveyard of slavery. I saw as utterly foolish and vain my hope of being reunited with my wife or of ever seeing my son.

I had, of course, been under scrutiny during the night and was still under scrutiny at early daybreak as I made my way slowly home, to be on hand for the driver's call to work. My bare back, for I could not suffer the weight of a shirt on the raw flesh, made a stark target in the half-light of false dawn. I vowed that kill me they might, but they would not kill me running. One shot would do the trick; "attempted escape" would be the perfunctory explanation.

I was incapable at the moment of caring whether I lived or died and would as soon the execution came. I no longer imagined myself to be a man and found it acceptable, having departed manhood, to depart life. I was like a drowning man, of whom it is said that his whole life passes in review as he struggles for breath in the inhospitable aqueous element. I saw my almost twenty-four years as a whole, and this was the sum of my years:

I am a slave. More than that, and infinitely worse, I am the father of a slave. A father has the duty and the right to rear his son from helpless infancy to manhood. Most deeply do I feel the duty of a father, but the right has been taken from me. My son is not mine.

What a desolate fate awaits you, my child! Shut out for life from every chance or hope of anything which makes it worth one's while to live—bred up a slave!

That single word slave speaks of chains, of whips and tortures, compulsive labor, hunger and fatigues, and all the miseries our wretched bodies suffer. It speaks of haughty power, insolent commands, avarice, purse-proud luxury, and of the indifference and scornful unconcern with which the oppressor looks down upon his victims.

And it speaks of fear, servility, and of low, mean cunning, and treacherous revenge. It speaks of humanity outraged, manhood degraded, the ties of father, wife, and child sundered and mocked. It speaks of aspirations crushed, hope extinguished, the light of knowledge sacrilegiously snuffed out.

It speaks of man deprived of all that makes him amiable or makes him noble, of man stripped of his soul and sunk into a beast and less than a beast.

To this fate, my child, thou art born.

May heaven have mercy on thee, for man has none.

Chapter 15

There was, truth to tell, an escape plot from Loosahachee planned for Christmas week, and not from Loosahachee alone; slaves from two of the neighboring plantations were involved. Rumors of slaves planning to escape during Christmas week are common throughout the South. Slaves will mumble their certainty of escape "come Christmas"; and fear and suspicion among the privileged class will serve to make slave plots a chief topic of conversation. Much of the talk is of plots that do not, in fact, exist.

But the plot among some of the slaves at Loosahachee, in concert with a few rascals from other plantations, was real and solid, and had promised to succeed because of its very simplicity. A number of slaves would, on a certain Christmas-week night, alone or in small groups, watch their chance and "disappear into thin air." They would go to ground in a certain cave, there to lie low until the hue and cry following their disappearance had died down. Then, at intervals, they would leave the hideout and make for the Barrens where upwards of half a hundred runaways lived the life of a gang of outlaws, pillaging the countryside for miles around. I later learned that the number fluctuated and that the "permanent residents" totaled not more than ten or fifteen. Theirs was a precarious existence, but infinitely to be preferred to the cruelty and cruel monotony of slavery.

It is customary, almost everywhere in the South, to allow slaves to have the week from Christmas to New Year's Day as a sort of holiday. They are given passes to visit friends and relatives, even though great distances may be involved; and slaves are allowed to wander about in their own neighborhoods much at their own will and pleasure. One of the great boons of Christianity for slaves is that their Christian masters are themselves in need of a week from slave-driving chores in order to celebrate the birth of the Saviour. They must perforce loosen a little the bonds of their captive converts and allow black Christians a degree of freedom for celebrating—in traditional ways similar to those of the masters —the birth of the gentle Jesus.

The highways at this season present a singular appearance. Slaves of every age and both sexes, dressed in the best attire they have been able to muster, assemble in great numbers. They crowd the roads or cluster about the little whiskey shops, presenting a lively scene of bustle and confusion seen at no other season of the year.

Not slaves only, but men generally, welcome the opportunity for merriment. And whenever their natural sources of enjoyment fail them, men will betake themselves to artificial excitements. It is only too evident that often we sing and dance, not because we are merry, but in the hope to become so. And merriment itself is less often the expression and the evidence of pleasure than it is the disguise of weariness and pain.

The merriment induced by liquor becomes more marked in the holiday season; and especially so among slaves, for drunkenness then is encouraged rather than frowned on or forbidden and severely punished. On the whole, slaves do not note a connection between relaxed discipline, the availability of watered-down whiskey at a dollar a quart, and the privilege of drinking themselves insensible without fear of reprisal or punishment. While relishing a taste of what seems to be something like freedom, the wretches spend their free time in dance or drugged torpor and let slip away what chance might exist for attaining real freedom. I have heard of a few who liquor-inflamed have staggered toward freedom—but of none who successfully completed a journey so inauspiciously begun.

Free men who will righteously condemn the slave for his so-called love of drink should remember that enslaved men will turn to anything which promises to sustain their sinking spirits and to excite their stagnant souls. They soon find in whiskey the something that seems to answer the purpose. In that elevation of heart which drunkenness inspires, that forgetfulness of the past and the present, that momentary halo with which it crowns the future, they find a delight which they hasten to repeat and know not how to forego. Reality is to them blank, dark, and dreary. Action is forbidden, desire

140

chained, hope shut out. They are obliged to find relief in dreams and illusions.

As for the escape plot this year at Loosahachee, it was because Jeff was part of the conspiracy that Thomas and I had heard of it. The reader will recall that on the *Two Sallys,* when the boarding party from the *Arethusa* had gone back to their ship with a promise to return, it was Jeff who had said, "There's time to eat before they get back." He had a sharp eye and a practical mind.

Jeff needed to tell no one the history of his life, for it could easily be read on his scarred body. He was of medium height, square-built, of a dusky copper color. He did not know the date of his birth. I suppose him to have been closer to Thomas' age (thirty years at the time) than to mine. He had been sent into the fields when he was perhaps eight years of age, and twenty years later bore scars on limbs, back, face, and head that bespoke innumerable batterings. An ugly, puckered M burned into his chest told of escape, capture, return to his master, and subjection to the branding which was intended to impress upon him that he belonged among the livestock.

He was a widely traveled man, having been frequently sold, and having seen much of the South by virtue of walking from place to place in chains. This man, with this history, had gravitated as if by instinct to the insurgent element at Loosahachee, and those brigands immediately recognized their brother.

Jeff had given us details of the Loosahachee escape plot as he learned them, and had informed us of the direction and location of the cave and of the long journey through trackless wilderness to the distant Barrens. He had had no hope, of course, that Thomas would join the runaways, for Thomas had believed escape to be a sin and that it was the moral duty of slaves to accept their lot as ordained by God. I had listened with interest to Jeff, for all that he said was as exciting to me as a tale of high adventure. But such was my regard for Thomas, and such my dread of the despair that would assail me if I had not his constant assurance that one day Cassy and I would be reunited, that I had never seriously considered leaving.

Women found Jeff attractive. He was the recipient of many a flashing glance from the bolder and more lively among them. He did not pursue the ladies, yet never need lack for a sweetheart. At Loosahachee he became the love target of Nellie, a scullery maid in the LeFavre household. Had this saucy young minx, perhaps eighteen years of age, not devoted most of her off-hours to attracting and holding Jeff's attention, these memoirs might here take a different turn or never have been written.

No passes were issued at Loosahachee on the Sunday following Ann's and the baby's burial. Some of the slaves congregated in quiet groups; others wandered restlessly; but the majority kept out of sight. Even children were scarce. Jeff and I made no effort to join any group, and no one sought our company. The slaves knew we were all closely watched. The fiendish public beatings administered to Jeff and to me had demonstrated that in Mr. LeFavre's view we possessed guilty knowledge of a most reprehensible kind. Any slave fraternizing with us would attract a like suspicion to himself. Nellie failed to make an appearance, for the house servants had been refused permission to visit friends and relatives among us.

Jeff and I at length sat down under a tree at some distance from any of the others, prepared to idle or sleep away the afternoon hours of a gray and muggy afternoon. I had suffered constant distress of mind for long days and nights, holding in check my apprehension about Thomas and my almost ungovernable urge to seek out the cave and learn whether he had found it and if he were there and alive or dead. But as often as I determined to learn the truth at all costs, I was deterred by the thought that if I made the attempt I could become the instrument of his betrayal. Besides, I was on occasion half convinced that Thomas had drowned on the watery way to the cave, whose location he knew of only by hearsay, and to reach which he had to cross terrain wholly unfamiliar to him.

"Look who is coming!" Jeff exclaimed. "We'll get a pretty preaching now!"

He slapped his knees, bent over, and broke into his characteristic laugh, an explosion of breath that was a series of gasps in reverse. I turned to see the old black parson making his purposeful way in our direction. I was more annoyed than amused at the prospect of a sermon from him. As for Jeff's amusement, I was accustomed to not understanding that. Often while working alongside him, I had heard his wheezing laughter and observed his shoulders shake in secret mirth. He seemed to carry on a succession of joking sessions with a number of private cronies. In some ways a strange fellow, Jeff had the attributes of true friendship; an ease in association and loyalty beyond question.

We greeted the parson civilly. The old gentleman waved his arms about as he exclaimed on the peace and beauty of God's Sabbath; he then clasped his hands, bowed his head, and launched into a fervent prayer for the salvation of our souls. The prayer changed in midstream and became a bizarre message that completely astonished me.

The parson said that Thomas had appeared to him in a vision. Thomas was in a cave, he said, and was well. He was recovering from a bullet wound in the upper arm. He had food and water. In the vision, Thomas had beseeched the parson to give his old friends this message: *Wait, and trust in the Lord.*

He pulled a tattered catechism from a pocket of his rusty black coat and appeared to read from it. He could not in fact read, but had memorized the catechism during the long years in which he had been given oral instruction from it. He prayed over us again, admonished us to come unto the Lord and be washed in the blood of the Lamb, and took his departure.

Jeff and I were overjoyed to learn from him that Thomas had located the cave, and we felt sure that he would rest patiently there, recovering from his wound, and that he would know that I, as well as Jeff, would be among those who would attempt to join him during Christmas week, scarcely two weeks hence.

We were both curious, however, as to the source of the old man's "vision," since we put scant credence in its supernatural origin. We concluded that one of the

144

conspirators from a neighboring plantation (one under less stringent restrictions than was Loosahachee) had seized an opportunity to visit the hideaway and had enlisted as messenger to us the one person at Loosahachee who Mr. LeFavre would not suspect of conspiratorial knavery.

Much relieved in our minds, and feeling better able to summon the patience to wait out the weeks remaining until Christmas, we stretched out to rest. Jeff soon dropped off to sleep, but sleep I could not. The paradoxical circumstance that the most trustworthy black man at Loosahachee had "scandalously" betrayed the trust implicitly placed in him by his master occupied my thoughts.

Dare Christian slaveholders learn the lesson to be read in our parson's "betrayal" (as they would call it)? Learn it they must if they intend to continue enslaving men! If they hope to bring their work in this nefarious business to the glorious completion they envision, let them prohibit at once *all* religious instruction.

Now, Christian slaveholders, in order to bring their avowals somewhat in line with their actions and thus ease their Christian consciences, allow slaves a jot and tittle, a mere glimpse of Christian faith and doctrine, through oral instruction from the catechism. Let me tell them that just here they make the first, fundamental, and fatal error.

Slaveholders ought to recollect that all knowledge is dangerous and that it is impossible to give slaves *any* instruction in Christianity without imparting to them some dangerous ideas. The catechism is nothing but the Bible in disguise. It matters not that the law prohibits

145

the teaching of slaves to read, thus making it impossible for them to read the word of God. Oral instruction in Christian precepts of love, compassion, mercy, and brotherhood are as dangerous as the written.

Let me tell them that the time is past in which the doctrine of passive obedience is all that a religious teacher has to say to the enslaved. Gentlemen, there is another spirit abroad and that spirit will penetrate wherever religious instruction of any kind opens the way for it. Nowadays it becomes increasingly impossible to acknowledge the slave a Christian brother without simultaneously acknowledging him a fellow man.

Another week passed. Leaden clouds lay close over us, stretching from horizon to horizon. In the heavy, still atmosphere, sounds carried long distances, and these muffled sounds—not generally heard in the fields and difficult to identify—carried threatening portents of danger. But what was the nature of the danger? When and from whence would it come? These unasked and unanswerable questions increased our apprehension. In this week there was constant low singing of hymns and work songs, taken up in one gang, dying away, and taken up again by another. These songs were simple, repetitious gibberish to white folk, who would cite the custom of singing at work as proof that slaves were contented and happy in their deadening toil!

Some of us were taken out of the field and for three days set to strengthening dikes, a task made necessary because the heavy rains upcountry had caused a rising of rivers, swamps, and bayous which, should it continue, would make the flooding of the countryside a possibility. Though strenuous and heavy, this labor was a welcome

146

change from the monotony and the oppressive atmosphere of work in the fields.

Jeff and I attended the parson's Sunday night prayer meeting, a regular weekly event we had not previously graced with our presence. It was after this meeting, and while I kept close to the parson in his peregrinations among the slaves (in the hope that he might have had another "vision" to report), that I noticed Jeff "walking out" with Nellie. Within the hour he had returned and, with a motion of his head, indicated I was to join him. On our walk in the general direction of our quarters, he repeated what he had learned from Nellie. Innocently, in a spate of gossip about what went on at the big house, Nellie told what she had overheard. What is overheard is usually only half heard and that half misunderstood, but we dared not ignore Nellie's information. Court was to be held at Loosahachee on Wednesday when the truth of the intended escape plot would be learned and the culprits identified and punished.

My fright and alarm at hearing this news was as great as was Jeff's. Our instinct was to take, heedlessly and recklessly, to our heels. Was this not an extreme reaction to news of a mere hearing? Before judging, let the reader remember that we were South Carolina slaves and that South Carolina justice (slavery justice) is not what Americans in general understand justice to be.

Let us examine slavery justice. The case, let us say, is this: One plantation owner has strong reason to suspect that his stores have been plundered by slaves from a neighboring plantation, or that he has been wronged because neighboring slaves have feloniously enticed his workers to join a black exodus to the North or to participate in a plot for insurrection and the cutting of every white throat in the neighborhood.

The wheels of slavery justice begin to turn. The overseer of the complaining neighbor visits the plantation, bringing with him his judge, jury, even executioner—and all in the person of three white freeholders of the district.

Three South Carolina freeholders selected at haphazard constitute such a court as, in most other countries in the world, would hardly be trusted with the final adjudication of any matter above the value of forty shillings, at the utmost. But in that part of our nation, they not only have the power of judging all charges, whether great or small, against slaves, but of sentencing the accused to death.

And what South Carolinians doubtless consider a much more important matter of impartial justice, in such a trial as this, is that the judges have the right of saddling the state treasury with the estimated value of the condemned culprit. The law states that the master is to be refunded a part of the value of the condemned, but a universal practice of overevaluation results in a refunding of what usually amounts to the full value. Thus the accused wretches are denied an important protection against an unjust sentence; for were the master in danger of suffering a sharp financial loss, he might find strong reason to come to the defense of his threatened property. Under this refunding law, accused slaves are left without any sort of shield whatever against the prejudice, careless indifference, or stupidity of their judges.

148

But why should we expect anything like equity or fairness in the execution of laws which themselves are founded upon the grossest wrong? It must be confessed that in this matter the Americans preserve throughout an admirable consistency.

Jeff and I knew without discussing the matter that we had already been tried, found guilty, and sentenced. We arranged to meet at a certain place no later than midnight. A hasty flight was necessary because by morning any opportunity for escape might have vanished. Was it not only because Christian masters hesitate to conduct worldly business on a Sunday that we had not already been taken up and held for trial? We parted. Three hours of the Sabbath remained.

It was to avoid the appearance of collusion that we made our separate ways to the meeting place; and in order not to attract attention, neither of us would attempt to approach others who might be suspected and tried. Whether the rumor of the trial had a basis in fact and had been transmitted widely through other informants than Nellie, would be revealed at daybreak when perhaps other drivers beside our own would fail to muster a full contingent when they called their victims out of the warrens.

Nellie did not know that her bit of gossip had put thoughts of immediate flight into Jeff's head. We determined that no one else should hear of our intent, not even our most trusted friends at Loosahachee, for the reason that we dared not risk our talk with others being noted and at once reported by those who might expect to profit from bearing tales. Why, among slaves themselves there are those who are regularly employed as spies and informers. It is impossible to know for a certainty who they are. That they exist is easily accounted for. Tyranny, whether on the great scale or the small, can be sustained only through a system of espionage and betrayal. In this way the most mean-spirited of the oppressed are turned into the tools and instruments of oppression. But consider how many alleviations of the wretchedness of his condition can be expected by the slave who earns the favor and indulgence of his overseer!

Let it be remembered, also, that so strong are the allurements which power holds out that even among free men there are hundreds of thousands always to be found who are ready to assist in sacrificing the dearest rights of their neighbors by volunteering to be the instruments of superior tyrants. What then can be reasonably expected from those who have been studiously and systematically degraded? What wonder if among the oppressed are found some of the readiest and most relentless instruments of oppression?

It cannot be said too often that *power is ever dangerous and intoxicating*. Human nature cannot bear it. It must be constantly checked, controlled, and limited, or it declines inevitably into tyranny.

Even the endearments of the family—connubial love and the heart-binding ties of paternity (and these strengthened, as they always are, by the controlling influence of habit and opinion)—even these precious endearments have not made it safe to entrust the head of a family with absolute power over his household! What terms then are strong enough in which to denounce the vain, ridiculous, and wanton folly of expecting anything but abuse where power is totally unchecked by either moral or legal control?

But I digress. Jeff and I parted, to wander idly about and each to watch for his opportunity to slip out of sight undetected. It was understood that if one was unable to meet at the appointed time, the other was to start out alone.

Chapter 16

Circumstances facilitated our escape. A goodly number of men had been withdrawn from guard duty at Loosahachee and on the roads and trails thereabouts, in part because of the lessening of the general panic following Thomas' escape, but also because the men were needed elsewhere. The danger of flooding in the countryside had increased, and workers were needed in the ditches and on the rice-field embankments.

I made slow and wary progress to the meeting place, saw no one, and arrived well ahead of the appointed time. I concealed myself and came out of deep cover only when I heard Jeff's low whistle.

"Something's on fire!" I exclaimed. Above the trees to the south, through misty air, a red glow flared and pulsated.

"I expect it's the neighbor's rice mill burning right down!" Jeff said.

It appeared that Jeff had spent the final Sabbath hours in ways more advantageous to our purpose than I. Men would be drawn from all directions by the conflagration, making it most unlikely that any would be on the lookout for runaways fleeing in the opposite direction.

We groped our way to the side of a rampaging creek and were able to make better time as we followed it upstream, for the rush of water covered our thrashing passage. At length we had to leave it and strike off across a flooded swamp. We constantly stepped into holes or tripped over submerged logs and were pitched sprawling into the ooze; but we floundered on, driving ourselves to the edge of exhaustion. After some hours of this I no longer believed that there was anywhere a firm spot of earth on which a man could rest.

Black night gave way at last to a gray atmosphere in which objects could dimly be seen. We had reached a thinly forested part of the swamp. We summoned the strength to strip some trees of their lower branches and heap them on the sodden and almost liquid turf. On this makeshift bed we slept—in filthy, sopping clothing that reeked of swamp—and slept soundly.

We were on our way again before midmorning and, at length, gained the narrow, swift river which carried on its crest branches, logs, barrel staves, and debris of every description. There followed a long interval of tramping miles up and down the bank as we searched for a certain arrangement of nature, on the opposite bank, that was said to mark the vicinity of the cave. Having found it, we raised our voices, calling Thomas and announcing ourselves. There was soon an answering shout, and the huge, bearded, black man emerged from the lush vegetation. He raised an arm in greeting. We raced upstream, plunged in, and swam, fighting to cross the strong current while it carried us down to Thomas.

Great as was our pleasure in seeing Thomas, we wasted few words on warm greetings. The circumstances of our meeting were these: The cave, in which we had supposed we would hide until Christmas week, was flooded. Thomas had wrapped his corn, rice, and salt in burlap, lashed the bundle with LeFavre's cowhide, and was only awaiting nightfall to move on. Since the cave was useless to us, we agreed to start out at once.

I was exultant and felt already free. We were going to put so many miles behind us that no posse, attempting to follow our trail through the hellish bog Jeff and I had somehow crossed, would be able to overtake us.

We had not left swamps behind. Oftentimes a swamp, or signs that we were too close to a plantation, caused us to deviate from the direction we wished to take. At the end of dismal hours of fog and fine drizzle, we encountered yet another bog and had before us the prospect of a long tramp around it. The wind had been steadily rising and now carried a chill foreboding of rain. We decided it was best, and safe enough, to build a rude shelter of some kind and to rest and restore our strength, through what promised to be a night of heavy wind and perhaps storm.

Suddenly I thought I heard, from the direction of our back trail, the sound most dreaded by the escaping slave.

"Listen!" I cried.

We kept silent. I was beginning to think that my ears, aided by my imagination and a trick of the wind, had played me false; but it came again, the distant baying of a hound. Again and again the animal gave tongue.

"It's Mister LeFavre's hound. It's Swamper," Thomas said. He loosed the whip, which had secured the bundle of food to his belt, and jammed the bundle inside his shirt. Jeff had a knife out. I searched for and found a lightweight stick with a gnarled end, a good enough cudgel.

The baying sounded at intervals, louder each time. "Where's the pack? He's alone, that Swamper. He's lost," Jeff said.

"LeFavre and Swamper must have got separated from the posse, thank God," I said. "But you can bet your bottom dollar that LeFavre's not far behind that damned dog."

We tramped in and out of the swamp, bent on confusing the hound and making it difficult for man or dog to determine whether we were in the swamp—or out of it and circling behind them. Jeff soon left us, saying, "I'll lay down a trail to draw him off from here."

Thomas and I were well concealed in the wooded marsh when the dog reached its edge. After some whining and confusion, he got Jeff's scent and went baying in pursuit. His last cry on this earth was a bloodcurdling snarl, abruptly cut off. After some minutes, Jeff rejoined us. Here is seen illustrated the necessity for the law, universal throughout the South, which makes it a crime for a slave to possess a knife, unless it is necessary to his work and is surrendered at the end of the workday.

My thought was that we must immediately bury

ourselves in the swamp, in the hope that we would, with luck and the coming of another black night, evade the mounted men and their dogs. I now saw that the posse had trailed us by anticipating our course; they had circled the immense bog Jeff and I had traversed so painfully, had crossed the river by bridge, and Swamper, at least, had found our scent. The others would soon backtrack, hit his trail, and be on us in full cry.

Thoughts of immediate flight were not, however, in Thomas' mind. He instructed me to climb a tree and keep watch. In answer to a signal from him, I was to yell to attract LeFavre's attention. He asked Jeff to follow him out of the swamp, after allowing a certain distance. I scrambled up the tree and found a perch that afforded a good view ahead and one from which I could also catch glimpses of Thomas and Jeff as they made their cautious and circuitous way to the edge of the swamp.

LeFavre emerged from the trees. He sat astride his horse for long minutes, his head lifted in an attitude of listening. He slowly walked the animal and peered down at the ground, looking no doubt for signs that Swamper had passed that way. Something attracted his attention. He dismounted in his clumsy way and bent for closer scrutiny. Thomas was, at this time, among the trees at LeFavre's back and drawing close to him.

LeFavre straightened, walked back to his horse, and was about to mount when, in answer to Thomas' raised arm, I uttered a series of loud shouts full of sound and words that made no sense, the whole meant to startle and confuse.

As if a lancet had pierced him, the fat man whirled

156

toward the swamp, clawing his pistol out of his pocket. A cowhide cut through the air, coiled about his neck, and jerked him off his feet as the pistol exploded. Thomas had not had a great deal of time to become adept in wielding the whip (wounded and sick as he was when he first found sanctuary in the cave), yet he had evidently occupied the short period of his convalescence in acquainting himself with the various and interesting properties of the cowhide, and in acquiring a certain skill in its use.

When I arrived on the scene, Jeff had the horse snubbed to a stump on which Jeff sat, idly honing his knife with a stone. Mr. LeFavre was bound to a tree with his own rope. Thomas stood before him, holding Mr. LeFavre's pistol loosely in one hand, the whip dangling from the other. Thomas said, "I say one time, I say one more time. Why did you whip a sick woman and a little young baby down to the ground and kill them?"

Terror had turned LeFavre's flesh to a color that nearly matched his eyes. The eyes darted like scampering white mice from Thomas to Jeff, or, more accurately, from knife to whip and gun. LeFavre's throat worked convulsively, but speech was beyond his power until I, a white-colored man, came up; for as all the world knows, white men are reasonable men and can be talked to.

LeFavre burst into speech. Allow me to sum up, as quickly as I may, what he said. Disgust prevents me from dwelling on the matter. He spent no time in trying to formulate an answer to Thomas' question. Conscious only of his dire peril, and believing that in me lay his only hope, he warned me first that his death would avail us nothing. We were sure to be caught. We were surrounded. Prolonged and hideous deaths were certain if we harmed the overseeer of one of General Wilbur-force's plantations.

We allowed him to spill his frantic thoughts, ourselves remaining silent. He kept on with threats and appeals, while Jeff continued to hone his knife and Thomas circled restlessly about, flicking vegetation with the whip.

At length, exhausted by terror and our ominous silence, the despicable creature burst into tears and asked what it was that we wanted? To get off scot-free? WAS IT OUR FREEDOM WE WANTED?

Very well, he would buy us! Yes, yes, not only would he buy me, but Thomas, too, crazed as he was! and Jeff. Yes, and give us a stake, too, for our expenses on the journey. It was well known, he said, that in the North niggers were as free as whites. More free! They as good as *owned* the North and lived off the fat of the land!

Fired by his idea, he urged me to talk it over with the others at once. They would see, he assured me, that if it were freedom they wanted, here it was, easy as pie, handed to 'em on a platter!

It was then that Thomas stepped out from behind the tree to which LeFavre was bound, put the pistol to the man's head, and fired. Thomas was a merciful man.

We took from LeFavre's possessions whatever was useful to us and easily transported: a little money from his pocketbook, his rope and pistol, and various articles from a saddlebag, including a hand axe, which I ap-

158

propriated, and a flask of whiskey (from which but a few nips had been taken), which Jeff put into his pocket.

Thomas stood looking at the corpse for some minutes. Since it was Thomas who stood thus, it is possible that the short vigil beside the body of his enemy was devoted to a silent intercession with the Lord for the everlasting peace of LeFavre's unholy soul. But it was with something like a sad contempt that Thomas, as he turned away, dropped the whip on the mound of lifeless flesh.

Our final task was to relieve the horse of all trappings and send it galloping back the way it had come, as free as the wind that whipped its mane like a banner.

We started out, but within the hour a storm, rapidly approaching, made it imperative for us to arrange shelter of some kind, against what threatened to be a night of gale and torrential rain. There was no longer need to flee dogs and men, who had probably long since given up the search. As soon as this had been stated, I felt assured that there had never been a posse. Neither Loosahachee nor any other plantation could spare men, in the flood emergency, to search for two foolhardy runaways. LeFavre alone had set out, armed with a vicious dog and a gun, to run down and kill Jeff and me. Was this not the desperate act of a tyrant who feels the reins of power slipping from his grasp? Why was it imperative for him to execute a death sentence *not yet pronounced* by judges at a trial—in a court not due to convene for yet another day!

Herein lies what makes somewhat comprehensible the otherwise incomprehensible murder of our dear Ann. She might have lived had her "discipline," so scandalously interrupted by her husband, not been completed at once with fiendish thoroughness. And the necessity for this cruel exhibition lies in the atrocious belief that troublemakers must be punished beyond reason or justice—solely to set an example for others who might be contemplating making trouble.

The authority of masters over their slaves is in general a continual reign of terror. Fear is the sole principle of human nature to which the slaveholder appeals. Slaves have been tried and *hanged* by judges who could not know, nor do I suppose that they much cared, whether the victims were innocent or guilty. Their great object was to terrify the survivors.

On the whole they succeeded. By making an example of some poor wretch, by summoning every slave on the plantation to witness a demonstration of "wholesome and necessary severity," the true purpose of slaveholding justice is accomplished. Slaves are deterred, for greater or lesser periods, from imagining themselves men and become outwardly the most abject of slaves and inwardly the most fear-ridden of men, the most bereft of hope.

That night Thomas, Jeff, and I were without fear, filled with hope and purpose. We were on our feet and moving. We were men and knew ourselves to be men.

Chapter 17

I have earlier described the extent of the Pine Barrens and its inhospitable aspect, and mentioned that runaway slaves lived there after a fashion, for shorter or longer periods. When we were once well within the Barrens, we were approached on several occasions by runaways who inquired from us whence we came and what our destination was. Sometimes one or another of them would share our fire and contribute roasting potatoes or a chunk of meat to our scanty fare. These individuals showed an odd mixture of friendliness and suspicion in their attitude toward us. The friendly interest was easily understood, for they were naturally desirous of news of the outside world. The suspicion was also natural; for what assurance had they that we were not spies, advance agents for a "sporting party?"

Sporting parties are made up of white men who find especially exhilarating the stalking and killing of other humans who, they say, must be exterminated as the most ferocious of wild predators. We had been in the Barrens scarcely a fortnight when one daybreak we

161

came upon the tragic evidence of this shocking "sport."

Four black men lay dead: three as if asleep beside the extinguished embers of a fire; the fourth slumped against a tree trunk farther off. He evidently had been the lookout, who had dozed at his post. There was evidence that a body of men had tied their horses in the woods; had approached and circled their victims as they slept; had each selected a target, taken aim with muskets, and at a signal fired simultaneously. The bodies were horribly mangled with buckshot. We scraped out a shallow trench and buried the murdered men.

Thomas had finished conducting a simple service when one of our new acquaintances, who from a distance had taken in the scene, came forward. He suggested that we rest through the day and accompany him that night on an arduous journey to a place where there would be plentiful food, good company, and certain safety from sporting parties who were evidently infesting our present neighborhood. Thus it was that we finally met the inner circle of the outlaw band and were welcomed among them. Further details of the hideaway, or of individuals in the band, will not be divulged in these pages. In the unlikely event that their "fortress" is ever discovered and attacked, let the attackers be warned that these brave men will die rather than be taken, and are well prepared to carry the greater part of any attacking party to the grave with them.

The men who killed the runaways we buried are *murderers*, and acknowledged to be so by the very state in which the crime was committed. By the law of South Carolina, the killing of a slave is regarded as murder.

It is probable this law has never been enforced (and would doubtless be treated by a jury of modern slave-holders as an old-fashioned and fanatical absurdity), yet there still lingers in the breasts of the people some remains of horror at the idea of deliberate bloodshed, and a sort of superstitious apprehension of the possible enforcement of this antiquated law. To blindfold their own consciences, and to avoid the possibility of a judicial investigation, each man of an attacking party leaves the scene alone, and none returns to ascertain how many have been killed or disabled. The poor wretches who are not so fortunate as to be shot dead upon the spot are left to the lingering torments of thirst, fever, starvation, and festering wounds. And when at length they die, their skeletons lie bleaching in the Carolina sun. Slavery is a desert. The civilizing and humanizing instincts of man wither under its hot blast.

Fugitives in the Pine Barrens lived in part on a supply of half-wild cattle which wander through the piney woods and feed on the coarse grass. The flesh is cut into long strips and dried in the sun. Thus cured, it is a palatable and nourishing food. It furnished a valuable item of barter with slaves from small plantations along the rivers, who were anxious to have it in exchange for corn and other produce pilfered from their masters' stores.

The wonder is not that so many slaves are accomplished thieves, but that more of them are not. The strongest, or almost the strongest, passion of the human mind is the desire for acquisition. This passion the slave can only gratify by plunder. Besides, such is the bane-

163

ful effect of slavery that it almost destroys the very germ of virtue. If oppression makes the wise man mad, it too often makes the honest man a villain. It embitters the feelings, and hardens and brutifies the heart. He who finds himself plundered from his birth of his liberty and his labors—his only inheritance!—becomes selfish, reckless, and regardless of everything save the immediate gratification of the present moment. Plundered of everything himself, he is ready to plunder in his turn—and even to plunder his brothers in misfortune.

Among the fugitives, a constant source of plunder was the widely separated small farms and plantations. Our depredations were carried out singly or in very small groups. As a general rule, we slept by day, usually with a guard posted, and prowled potato and corn plantings by night. A long and arduous trip, but one regularly undertaken, was the journey to a distant white trader who accepted cattle hides in exchange for whiskey, and no questions asked.

This life, at least at first, seemed full of interest and had a certain charm of novelty about it. Freedom was the great compensation, even though it was a savage and stealthy freedom, filled with hardships and dangers.

Jeff and I had not long been reunited with Thomas, before we knew that he had changed in an important way, in that he had become two men. The second had been born early in the lonely, suffering hours following his escape. He had not needed to be told of Ann's and the baby's deaths. Ann had appeared to him in the cave and had told him that she and the baby were with God and were at peace; that he was not to mourn, for

164

they would all three be together throughout eternity.

Ann was often with Thomas in the Pine Barrens. He was given to wandering off and to talking to himself (or perhaps to Ann), unaware that on occasion he was overheard by Jeff and me. Certain incidents etch themselves on the mind, and such a one is the following: We three friends were scraping an ox hide and had fallen silent, intent on our work, when Thomas said, "Yes. They're at peace at the right-hand side of God. All the dead people in the whole world, they come up and God says, 'Come here, children, on the right-hand side, and rest in the glory of God.'"

Jeff's head came up. "All people? Archy and Jeff?" We two had no illusions about our names being inscribed in the golden book kept by angel scribes.

"All people." Over Thomas' eyes had fallen the curtain of inward seeing. "All the tribes . . . the multitudes . . . all the souls, they're with God forever."

Jeff's skepticism was deep. "LeFavre, now. Is *he* at the right-hand side of the Lord?"

Thomas nodded and bent to his work, still deep in his own inner world and unaware of us.

Jeff leaned toward me. "Archy, there's one fellow off to the left-hand side—the devil. He jumps up and down, and hollers, 'Hand over some of the people for this big fire I got burning here, Lord.' But the Lord, he holds out his strong left arm. He holds off that devil. Hah!"

Thus, in consigning to heaven every mortal soul— every soul who had ever lived or now lived or waited to be born—Thomas had inadvertently added another entertaining act to Jeff's interior vaudeville, one in

165

which the devil screamed and clawed and kicked and bit at the Lord's strong left arm and got nowhere, but only made a bigger damned fool of himself. I sometimes run that turn across the boards in the stage of my mind, and I smile and feel a certain satisfaction.

The excitement, the sheer physical effort, and the mental and nervous alertness necessary for survival in Pine Barrens allowed me for a time to accept the mournful fact that Cassy and my son were dead to me. But as the novelty of the new life wore away, as its miseries and alarms acquired a pall of monotony, my thoughts returned again and again to my family, and to freedom. I resurrected Cassy and little Archy from slavery's graveyard, where I had, in utter hopelessness, interred them. In my imagination I searched for them and found them and carried them off to freedom.

To accomplish my purpose, I must first get to the North, where blacks were "as free as whites" and could work, earn, and acquire wealth. I devised a number of schemes for finding my loved ones, but the one I favored was to return to the South in the guise of an agent for a dying, wealthy lady who had once owned a light-skinned maid named Cassandra, and who would pay a high price to have the dear girl once again under her roof, to attend her on her deathbed. I was sure that this plan offered the best chance for success, appealing as it did to the cupidity of those inured in the belief that fellow beings are articles of commerce, and who operate under what amounts to a moral imperative to turn a nice profit on slaves.

I found my tongue. I was full of the North and of freedom. As a result of talking in this vein whenever a

166

group gathered, I was led to consider ideas others expressed, and as a result, altered my plans in some degree. Those who had on occasion given thought to making the fearful dash to freedom, dreamed of reaching a place I had never heard of. It was called Ontario, more northerly than North, and freer. I was brought to reflect that a fugitive in the North was subject to being caught out and returned to slavery. Jeff had just such a tale to tell. So it was that Ontario, in Canada, a country which harbored fugitive slaves, became my destination. Men seated about dying campfires, in what I esteemed the place most forsaken of God in the universe, a gang of the rudest fellows anywhere to be found, talked of the freedom to be enjoyed, not in their own native land but in a monarchial country bordering the vaunted free American democracy!

At this bleak time of year, there was a general thinning of the human population of the Barrens; because of a dwindling in the supply of starving cattle, men ranged farther afield in search of food. Many failed to return, their fate—good or bad—unknown to us. I had determined that the time had come for me to push on and had persuaded Thomas and Jeff to accompany me. They had experienced a few months of the comparative safety and freedom of the Barrens and were not as anxious as was I to quit the place forever. But my boundless faith in the proposition that we would eventually gain true freedom, had at last, it seemed, won them over. We were fortunate in that we had at hand a guide in the person of one Cunis. After a year of freedom, he longed to return to his home country, north of the Santee. He had a wife and little ones there and was assailed with homesickness. The country, he said, abounded with herds of fat cattle, which were easily plundered of strays.

After a journey of nearly two weeks, through piney country and abrupt and sudden sandhills, Cunis left us. Before doing so, he sketched in the dirt a map of our location, and the way we must take to reach Camden and the great northern road leading from that town into North Carolina.

My thoughts were constantly taken up with my plans for travel through the slave states. I would go as a tramp, an orphaned poor white. But to put a better face on the matter, I would give out that I had a relative, an uncle, who owned a store in New York City, and that once I reached that place I would find respectable employment with him. As one temporarily down on his luck, but with a laudable goal in mind, I hoped to elicit more help and sympathy than if I traveled as one who tramped by choice. Such footloose and ambitionless fellows are despised and not a little feared by the more orderly members of society. I would try to earn my way by doing odd jobs or by begging, and would endeavor to refrain from practicing my thieving skills, for I dared not invite warranted suspicion and the close scrutiny that would follow. Thomas and Jeff must also refrain from plunder. "I will travel openly and scrounge enough for all. At night we will meet to divide the spoils," I told them.

I attempted to change my appearance to the degree possible to me. General Wilburforce was one of the wealthiest and most powerful men in the Carolinas. It was to be expected that he would advertise widely for the men who had killed his Loosahachee overseer and in "impudent defiance" had draped the corpse with the man's own whip. How many hundreds, even thousands, attracted by the huge reward offered on a WANTED poster had memorized our descriptions and already made plans how they would spend the money?

I hacked off my crisp curls close to the scalp and covered my head with a filthy cotton cap. Such hair as mine is a matter for speculation in the South where, among a certain class of people, detection of "nigger blood" is an obsession that is building a canon of immutable laws from which there is no appeal, because embedded in ignorant superstition and prejudice. In the past months Thomas had grown a full and luxuriant beard. Jeff and I, lacking genius in this respect, had for the most part kept our spare whiskers scraped off. In the last weeks, however, I had allowed a sparse and wispy beard to grow. Its great virtue as a disguise was that it was but slightly curly and was not brown but of a decided reddish hue.

Toward evening one day, we judged ourselves to be close to the rough road that would lead us to Camden and the highroad beyond. We settled down in a thicket, made a meal of dried beef, and prepared to rest and laze away the long hours until daybreak.

In a jocular mood, I said, "You'd never know me for Archy Moore, the slave, now would you, boys?"

They agreed that my disguise was a good one. But Jeff said that if I were ever to be seen in company with them "the jig would be up" with me. "There's no disguising *us*," said he. It was true. There was no disguising Jeff's badly scarred, coppery face. As for Thomas, his

169

size and commanding presence would always set him apart and fix him in the memory of any who caught a glimpse of him.

My two friends then told me, in kindly and earnest tones, that they would not be going on with me, but next day would turn back and once again seek safety in the Barrens. Thomas said that later in the year he would return to the vicinity of Loosahachee, for he had never visited the grave of his wife and child.

Greatly agitated, I attempted to speak, but the words of persuasion and argument I might have used died in my throat. I saw the true situation, which was that they had never entered wholeheartedly into my plans; my good friends had come this long way with me only to encourage and strengthen me in my purpose. It is impossible to know which caused me greater agony: the prospect of going on alone, or the glimmering their words gave me of their expectations for their own future. They anticipated living forever at the edges of civilization, forever hunted as outlaws, forever subject to capture and summary execution. They embraced the freedom available to them and had lost all hope for anything better.

I parted from my friends early next morning at the edge of the woods bordering the rutted track leading to Camden. Jeff said to watch out sharp, keep my shirt on, and I'd do just fine on my journey. Thomas, too, gave me encouraging words, embraced me, and said, "Go now, and God go with you." He released me, turned abruptly, and he and Jeff disappeared among the mist-enshrouded trees.

Thus we parted. As I hastened toward Camden, I saw

myself once again as Ishmael, though not the despairing and anguished Ishmael of my youthful years. If I were close to tears as I waded through drifts of knee-high fog, it was a scalding, impotent anger that summoned them.

I was not only Ishmael, but doubly Ishmael—cast out at birth from my father's people and now an outcast from my mother's people, also. I had embarked on a career of passing for white, wherein I would deny my people over and over again and claim not to know of them. I was putting behind me the "peculiar institution" that men had structured for millions of their dark-skinned brothers, the system that so cruelly demeans and imprisons them and their children and their children's children through all their generations.

Nay, worse than this, our tyrants are industriously engaged in arranging that we wander as outcasts *throughout eternity.* A close examination of their words, actions, and policies concerning us will reveal the truth of this scandal.

Now have we not seen how Mr. Carleton of Carleton Hall did most sincerely believe (and the immense majority of his fellow countrymen join him in the belief) that the Bible contains a revelation from God of things essential to man's *eternal* welfare? Have we not seen how devout philanthropists contribute their money very liberally so that every family in the country may have a copy of the Bible, the divine and unerring guide? But they withhold it from their slaves (of whom, to use their own hypocritical cant, God has appointed them the natural protectors)—*and in so doing expose those slaves to the danger of eternal punishment!*

To this awful danger they voluntarily and knowingly

171

expose them lest should the wretches learn to read, they might at the same time learn something of their own rights and the means of enforcing them.

What outrage upon humanity was ever equal to this?

Other tyrannies have gone to great lengths to insure that there shall be no earthly happiness for their victims. But what other tyrants are recorded, in all the world's history, to have openly and publicly confessed that they prefer to expose their victims to the imminent danger of eternal damnation, rather than impart a degree of instruction which might—just possibly—endanger their own unjust and usurped authority? Can anyone calmly consider this diabolical avowal and believe that it is *Christian* men who make it? And men, too, who seem in other matters not destitute of the common feelings of good will and who speak of liberty, virtue, religion, even of justice and humanity!

Are they men or devils who put on a semblance of human feelings in order the more secretly and securely to prosecute their grand conspiracy against mankind? I should believe them devils, did I not know that the love of social superiority, which is the mainspring of civilization and the chief source of all human improvement, is able (when suffered to work on, uncontrolled by other more generous emotions) to corrupt man's whole nature and drive him to acts most horrid and detestable.

When a corrupt passion for superiority is joined to a base and cowardly fear, its victim is to be pitied rather than hated. The maniac can hardly be held accountable for the enormities to which his madness prompts him, even though that madness is self-created.

172

Chapter 18

Had my skin been black, I might here have been able to record a tale of alarms, dangers, pursuits, and hairbreadth escapes as I made my way across North Carolina, Virginia, and Maryland. Such a journey, for a lone black man having neither friends nor money to ease his way, and unable to so much as inquire concerning roads and directions without arousing suspicion, is a most desperate, even suicidal, undertaking.

For my part, traveling as poor white trash, I was alternately suspected of being a thieving vagrant, the pathetic orphan I proclaimed myself to be, a shiftless no-account who chose to beg rather than work for a living, a young fellow who, although disreputable, seemed to deserve a helping hand, or a probable criminal just a few steps ahead of pursuing lawmen. My poverty and state of homelessness was an offense to a great many, whose main hope in regard to me was that I might speedily take myself out of sight and mind.

There were, on the whole, more kindly white people, both men and women, than I had expected to encounter.

In Maryland, while I was stacking cordwood I had split, the young farmer came from the barn, after his chores there were finished, and pitched in to help me finish the job. My supper was set out on the kitchen table. The man sat with me as I ate, while his wife busied herself putting their young children to bed. He said I should make myself comfortable in the hayloft that night—a blanket would be provided—and that he could doubtless find enough work to keep me busy for a week about the place. He said he would pay some little money in addition to bed and board.

When he asked how conditions were in Virginia, I reported them as bad. What work a man could sometimes find, I told him, did not pay enough to keep him decently alive.

He shook his head. "It's the slave labor," he said. "But I wouldn't buy me a slave, even if I had the money. It ain't right to work a man lifelong for no pay—that's what I say. Young fellows like you, now, have to get theirselves up North, and why is that? 'Cause at home here there's slaves doing work *for no pay* that young fellows like you could do to earn theirselves a stake. The whole thing's rotten, from top to bottom—that's what I say. Not that saying does much good. I might's well holler down a rain barrel. Nothing's going to change."

I left the barn as soon as the moon rose. I fled from a man who I felt to be so sympathetic to me, in spirit and outlook, as to present a real danger, in that I would be tempted to "holler down a rain barrel" with him on a subject that greatly concerned me but which concern I dare not reveal to anyone. My life and freedom were at stake.

174

Nevertheless, this decent man's views had an effect on my own. Although he had not so stated the proposition, the tenor of his remarks led directly to the conclusion that slavery was so bad a system (and not for slaves only, but for the ordinary free citizens of the South) that it should be done away with altogether. I had not before heard anyone speak in quite so forthright a manner concerning the peculiar institution.

Major Thornton I had heard fulminate against the *abuses* of slavery. And he had in his own way tried to ameliorate the worst conditions among the people he owned. There are other slaveowners who are kind and benevolent, each after his own fashion. And do we not know that through the broad extent of slaveholding America there are, without doubt, many amiable women and good mistresses?

Yet how little does their kindness avail! It reaches only here and there. It has no power to alleviate the wretchedness or to diminish the tortures of myriads of wretches who never hear a voice softer than the overseer's and who know no discipline milder than the lash.

Such is the malignant nature and disastrous operation of the slaveholding states, that in too many instances the sincerest good will and best intended efforts in the slave's behalf end only in plunging him into deeper miseries. It is impossible to build any edifice of good on so evil a foundation. The whole system is totally and radically wrong.

The benevolence, the good nature, the humanity of a slaveholder, avail as little as the benevolence of the bandit who generously clothes the stripped and naked traveler in a garment plundered from his own port-manteau.

What grosser absurdity than the attempt to be humanely cruel and generously unjust!

The very first act in the slave's behalf, without which all else is useless and worse than useless, is *to make him free.*

My long and tiresome walk through three Southern states blends into a memory of wretched and lonely roads that led me through a vast, monotonous extent of unprofitable woods and deserted fields grown up with broom sedge and mullen, or past fields just ready to be deserted (so gullied and barren were they), and with all the evidences upon them of a negligent, unwilling, and unthrifty cultivation. Here and there I passed a mean and comfortless house. Once in fifty miles I came upon a decaying, poverty-stricken village, with a court-house, a store or two, and a great crowd of idlers collected about a tavern door, but nowhere a single sign of industry and improvement.

I always, for safety's sake, put myself among this class, as a man who knows his place and naturally drifts into it. I never spoke more than was necessary, content to give the appearance of an exceptionally stupid fellow, and never entered into what goes for "conversation" among these people. It may be that it was the restraint I put myself under, in thus holding my tongue, that caused me so to dislike the company of these fellows, and to escape from them as speedily as I could.

The condition of poor whites is distressful in the extreme. They are rude, ignorant, and acquainted with but few of the comforts of civilized life. They are idle, dissipated, and vicious, with all the vulgar brutality of vice which their poverty and their ignorance render so conspicuous and disgusting.

They have no land, or at best possess some little tract of barren and exhausted soil which they have neither the skill nor the industry to render productive. They are without trade or handicraft. They look upon all manual labor as degrading to free men and fit only for the state of servitude. These poor whites have become the jest of the slaves, and they are feared and hated by the select aristocracy of rich planters.

What preserves for these wretches the degree of consideration and respect with which they are yet treated is the right of suffrage. This right (of which the select aristocracy is extremely anxious to deprive them) is the only safeguard of the poor whites. Without this the force of law and legislation would soon reduce them to a condition little superior to that of the very slaves themselves.

I avoided Baltimore (city of slave pens and port of embarkation for American slave ships plying our coastal waters) and crossed into Pennsylvania. I had scarcely passed the slaveholding border before the change became apparent.

The spring was just commencing, and everything was beginning to look fresh, green, and beautiful. The nicely cultivated fields, the numerous small enclosures, the neat and substantial farmhouses thickly scattered along the way, the pretty villages and busy towns, the very roads themselves, lively with the passage of wagons and foot travelers—all these signs of universal thrift

177

and comfort gave me abundant evidence that at length I saw a country where labor was honorable and where everyone labored for himself. It was an exhilarating and delightful prospect to me, so strong was the contrast with all I had seen in the previous part of my journey.

One early morning, somewhere in Pennsylvania, I bathed in a stream, using a chunk of strong lye soap I carried with me. I scraped my face clean of the beard. I washed my shirt, spread it on a bush to dry in the breeze and the warming rays of the rising sun, and spent the interval, waiting for it to dry, in paring my nails and in cutting and combing my unruly hair into some kind of order.

What I saw of myself reflected in the stream was not the prettiest picture in the world. But it would have been a grand one, had my nondescript features outwardly displayed the inward pride and pleasure I now took in myself.

When a man must, to preserve his very life, accept pity and compassion, while knowing himself to be neither pitiable nor the object of either a sentimental or a truly felt compassion; when he must invite insult and scorn, and be unable to defend himself against them or deny their cruel validity; when he must purposely present himself to his fellows as belonging among the lowest and most offensive order of men, until at last he becomes an offense in his own nostrils; when he must announce himself as a man lacking in even a suggestion of the normal pride, dignity, and wholesome self-assurance and self-reliance which are the hallmarks of manhood—when such a man can, then, feel that he has quite washed away shame and despicable, lying pretense, is that day not one to celebrate with rapture?

My exultation was not so great as to blind me to the sober truth that, although I had crossed into the North, I was by no means free. I had yet a long way to go, another border to cross, one that would separate me from slavery—and from my native land—forever. I resumed my journey, determined to watch my step— to keep my shirt on, as Jeff had advised—and to reach that border.

I was desirous of seeing Philadelphia. But that city, so near the Maryland border, I feared might be infected with something of the slaveholding spirit, for the worst plagues are the most apt to be contagious. I passed by, without passing through it, and hastened on to New York.

I crossed the noble Hudson and entered the town, the first city worthy to be called a city that I had ever seen. I was astonished and delighted when I beheld the spacious harbor crowded with shipping, the long lines of warehouses, the numerous streets, the splendid shops, and the crowds of energetic people. To my rustic in-experience the city seemed almost interminable. The rattling of the drays and carriages over the pavements, and the crowds of people in the streets, far exceeded all my previous notions of the busy confusion of a city. I was struck with the idea which all this gave me of the resources of human art and industry. I had heard of such things before, but to *feel* one ought to *see*.

I lingered in New York City for three days. True, I had renounced my country, if indeed that place can

179

fitly be called one's country which, while it gives him birth, cuts him off by its wicked and unjust laws from everything that makes life worth living.

A virtual war raged within me. My mind it was that had renounced my country. But now, having come so far and with my goal almost within reach, I experienced an unexpected attachment for my native land. Yet to remain in the "free" North would be to subject myself to capture and return to the South under the atrocious Fugitive Slave Law; and should such a catastrophe occur, I would by my own cowardly action consign my wife and child to slavery forever.

It happens to mankind in general that it takes a long time for a man to learn to compare, to weigh, and to judge. So strong were my emotions that I cannot rightly say what I thought as I wandered about the harbor on the third day of my stay. I was shaken with a savage fury and a passionate desire for revenge. I was a slave and felt the fierce spirit and ferocious energy of the slave who is at last driven to vindicate his liberty at sword's point, one who looks upon the slaughter of his oppressors almost as a debt due to humanity. Yet what of the nature of the justice won through passion, bloodshed, and the fury of blind and pitiless revenge? Thoughts and feelings such as these warred within me.

What an abundance of folly and falsehood about my country—a country founded on liberty, justice, equality, where each man was free to pursue happiness!—yes, what *lies* had been palmed upon me under the sober disguise of truth. And that, too, by my own father as I attended him and his friends at dinner. It was from Colonel Charles Moore I had heard those ringing words spoken for America and liberty that so moved my heart and fired my young mind. And this man was a paragon of the honorable Virginia gentleman.

Most dishonorable of men, he could deliver the most high-minded and chivalric remarks concerning women, while at the same time basely dishonoring womanhood. He was admired for his strict observance of that code of conduct toward women in which he had been educated. To have made an attempt on the chastity of a neighbor's wife or daughter he would have esteemed, and so the code of the Virginia gentleman esteems it, an offense that can be expiated only by the offender's life.

But beyond this, Colonel Moore did not dream of prohibiting or restraining his warm and voluptuous temperament. He was hardened and emboldened in this by his knowledge that he could suffer no harm nor loss, provided the sufferer were a slave. He regarded the most atrocious outrage that could be perpetrated upon the person and feelings of a slave woman as a matter of jest—a thing to be laughed at over the fourth bottle, rather than a subject of serious and sober reprehension.

What bitter anguish was mine to know that my wife's happiness and well-being rested with such honorable gentlemen as Colonel Charles Moore! For the sake of my sanity, I constantly reassured myself that it was more likely than not that Cassy had become the property of some good and kind woman, that she and our boy were well and even affectionately treated. Have I said how little avails the kindness of kind mistresses, that it reaches only here and there? May it reach my wife and child and preserve them for me, until I can bring them out of slavery and under the protection of husband and father! While scattered good deeds can avail little in relieving the miseries of millions in bondage, to the individuals upon whom such blessings fall, they are worth, not little—but the world.

Purposeful action will ever prevent the mind from preying on itself and poisoning itself with bitter recollections, and so it happened with me. Toward the end of an afternoon of wandering about the harbor, I decided that I would at once set out to seek the north road leading to Connecticut and, eventually, to Canada. I turned abruptly from the harbor, and with firm steps and a mind calm in its resolve, I started down a street of small shops I did not remember having traveled before. In turning that corner, I turned my life around.

Chapter 19

I had stopped for a moment to examine merchandise set out in bins for sidewalk display. The owner came out, greeted me pleasantly, and began hauling at one of the bins, with the evident intention of pulling it inside. "Let me give you a hand, sir," I said.

Without describing this man, his store, or his merchandise, I will here sum up our interchange, and the momentous consequences to me of this chance meeting. His helper had "run off to sea" that very morning. While I helped with the bins, the closing of shutters, and other lock-up duties, I noticed that he questioned me closely, and I sensed that he might be considering offering me the job so recently vacated by his harumscarum helper. He was a forthright fellow, saying that he could tell that I had some schooling and, to judge by my speech, had but recently arrived from the South. I admitted as much.

"You're well acquainted with slavery, then. Let me tell you, in the North we consider it an abomination, pure and simple. What's your opinion, may I ask?"

I had never before been asked my opinion on the subject. "Why, it's rotten from top to bottom and ought to be wiped off the face of the earth!" I said. I enjoyed this frank exchange. "But it's fixed solid, sir, in the South, and nothing's going to change it. So why holler about it? Might's well holler down a rain barrel!"

He leaned against a cupboard, folded his arms across his chest, and gave the impression of a man settling down to a long discussion. "I'm surprised to hear a Southerner speak as you do. I know there are people in the South unhappy with slavery. But they are few— precious few!"

"On the contrary, sir, most of the people in the South would be glad to see every slave set free immediately— at once—tomorrow morning, if possible!"

"Why, how can you say so? You must be jesting!"

I saw that in my exhilaration I had quite inadvertently shocked him into indignation, and was sorry for it. I hastily explained that I was indeed jesting and exaggerating, and on a subject too serious to permit playful remarks. I said in apology, "It went through my head that close to half the Southerners are black, and—it is *those* Southerners I refer to, sir."

This brought a rueful headshake. He then came out with his offer to hire me. He explained the duties of the job and the modest salary he would pay. The bed and chest of drawers in the back room would be mine; my meals I would take with the family. A decisive and energetic fellow, he stepped quickly into the back room, to call up the stairs and ask his wife to set out an extra plate for supper. I had heard the domestic sounds of hurrying footsteps and children's voices from the upper rooms, and had sniffed the aroma of what I guessed to be a stew. "There's a pump out back, for washing up. Take your time, think it over, and we'll talk again after supper," he said when he rejoined me.

I was sorely tempted to accept the man's offer. But, of course, I could not. I could not stay in New York under the constant threat of being picked up as a fugitive. Neither could I allow this honest and decent man to risk the danger of harboring a fugitive.

I mumbled, trying to refuse with some mealymouthed excuse, while also trying to express my heart-felt gratitude for his offer, which revealed a greater trust in me than I had in myself. I felt a great urge to trust him, in turn, with the truth. I unbuttoned my shirt, and as I hastily pulled it off, I turned about to show him my back and the ugly, disfiguring scars I would carry throughout my life.

I faced him and said, "I am a Negro and a slave. You would be harboring a fugitive. And as for me, sir, I am sick to death of skulking about! Thank you, but I'll continue on to Ontario, where a man can be free."

I was content to suffer the silence that fell between us and calmly met the look of bewilderment and disbelief on the man's face. Indeed, I felt some little sympathy with what must have been his alarm at having almost committed a rash action which would have jeopardized his safety, his livelihood, and the very welfare and happiness of his family.

It was he who broke the silence. "I see the hand of God in this!" he exclaimed.

As I bring these memoirs to a close, my son is in his

fifth year. I had planned that by this time my pockets would be stuffed with Canadian gold and I would be traveling among Southern plantations, inquiring for Cassandra and young Archy; inquiring too, for a couple of renegades called Thomas and Jeff. Instead, I am a poor American, but for all that closer to finding my wife and son and even my fugitive friends, than I would be if I were a veritable Croesus.

In almost every American city, town, and hamlet are free Americans, black and white, who insist on acting justly despite unjust laws which make their actions criminal. In the North, in some Border States, and yes, even in the South these friends of humankind do not run to ground the terrified wretches fleeing tyranny. They seek them out, lift them up, feed, clothe, shelter them, and speed them on to safety.

And to each one coming out of slavery, questions are put concerning others still wandering in that graveyard: "Do you know ____?" "Have you heard of ____?" Some day—it may be tomorrow—someone will answer a certain question, saying, "Cassy and the boy Archy? I've seen those people!"

Wife!—thou hast yet a husband who has not forgotten, and cannot. Child!—thou hast yet a father, one who will not forsake thee. I await our reunion with confidence.

The wealth of America is not, as some boastful patriots will maintain, in her rich cotton harvests, her textile mills and manufactures, her profitable exports, her internal slave trade, her fleets of ships, her teeming towns, nor in the rich promise of her vast, unpeopled territories. Her wealth is in her people, who, half a

186

century after the great Revolution of 1775–83, which freed her of one tyranny, will again risk danger, treasure, even life itself, to throw off another. Though poor, I am wealthy in these people. When slavery will end for all, I do not know. But it cannot survive as an institution among those who declare it to be self-evident that "all men are created equal."

This I maintain, regardless of knowing full well that the streets of Northern cities are infested with agents and owners who in their search for fugitive slaves are given enthusiastic cooperation by Northerners. And are there not Northerners regularly displaying a repellent eagerness to rid the North of *every* black man, be he fugitive or free? These fellows cry "fugitive" on the flimsiest of excuses.

Certain lawyers, Negro and white, doggedly turn up in police stations and in courtrooms and endeavor to speak for the ensnared black man, who is too often as terrified, as degraded, and as ignorant as the most debased of the enslaved in the South. Standing at the back of a crowded courtroom during such a trial, I have heard angry murmurs concerning the white lawyer that he was "no better than a nigger himself and ought to be given his walking papers"; and of the black advocate for a black brother, "He's one of them tricky niggers— ought to be rode out of town on a rail!"

Yet in the same courtroom, on a different occasion, when a fugitive had been sentenced to return to the South, I heard a rising protest of "Shame! For shame!" until the worthy judge must needs cry for order and threaten dire consequences to all who so disgracefully disrupted the dignity and decorum of a court of law!

Thus were these good Christians subdued and cast into confused and unhappy silence.

Alas, Christianity! What avails thy concern for the poor, thy tenderness for the oppressed, thy system of fraternal love and affection! Tyrants of every age and country have succeeded in prostituting Christianity into an instrument of their crimes, a terror to their victims, and an apology for their oppressions. Nor have they ever wanted for timeserving priests and lying prophets to applaud, encourage, and sustain them!

Another scene I have witnessed is this: A fugitive in custody of a law officer and on his way to jail gave a sudden spring and tore himself from the officer's grasp. He darted through the crowd, which opened to give him passage and closed to block the way of the furious and cursing officer. "Stop, thief!" cried a citizen on the outskirts of the throng. His accusation displayed a great ignorance of what was afoot. But it is common practice to charge a Negro with theft. He is automatically assummed to be guilty because, as everyone knows, "They are all thieves." And no matter how vehemently he protests his innocence, he is still guilty, for as everyone knows, "They are all liars."

Within two hours my employer and his friends had located the fugitive of the above incident, and within twelve hours he was on his way to safety farther north.

Thanks are due for this man's escape to the good will of the citizens of New York. Other mobs, on other days, will assist officers in pummeling their defenseless prey into submission, and will outdo one another in heaping vicious invective on their hapless victims.

In trying to account for civic turmoil of this nature,

must we not look first to the laws and the men who make them? The secret bias and selfish interest of the lawmakers often lead them wrong. Those who try to enforce such laws are aided and abetted by the artful practice and cunning instigation of purchased friends and bribed advocates of oppression. Their base interests are joined with the interest that the thieves and pickpockets of a great city always have in civil tumult and confusion. It is to the selfish interest of too many men to encourage, rather than quell, civil disturbance. And it is all too often the case that they succeed in exciting the young, the ignorant, the thoughtless, and the depraved to acts of violence in favor of tyranny. But so congenial to the human heart is the love of freedom that it burns not brighter in the souls of sages and of heroes than in the bosoms of even the most ignorant and thoughtless—when not quenched by some excited prejudice, base passion, or sinister influence.

I find that the most fortunate circumstance of my childhood was the opportunity to acquire a smattering of education and a foretaste of the excitements and joys which the pursuit of knowledge holds. It was this which opened for me opportunities for expanding my life in all the important ways which, for ignorant men, are nonexistent and unimaginable.

In the last two years I have, through books, traveled the world and talked with men in every corner of it. And while I have not myself traveled, I have—in concert with the men with whom I work—learned much of other countries and civilizations, as reported by returned travelers. Through books, through lectures, and in conversations with men wiser and more widely traveled than I, I have been to virtually every country in Europe and have learned much of various schemes of society, of their laws, and of their manners.

Everywhere I have seen the hateful empire of aristocratic usurpation, lording it with a high hand over the lives, the liberty, and the happiness of men. But everywhere, almost without exception, I have seen the bondsmen beginning to forget the base lore of traditional subserviency and beginning to feel the impulses, and to lisp in the language, of freedom. I have seen it everywhere—*except in my native America.*

There are slaves in many other countries but nowhere except in America is oppression so heartless and so unrelenting. Nowhere else has tyranny ever assumed a shape so fiendish, because nowhere else is it the open aim of the laws and the professed purpose of the masters to blot out the intellects of half the population and thus to extinguish at once and forever both the capacity and the hope of freedom.

In Catholic Brazil and in the Spanish islands, where one might expect to find tyranny aggravated by ignorance and superstition, the slave is still regarded as a man and as entitled to something of human sympathies. He may kneel at the altar by his master's side. He may hear the Catholic priest proclaiming boldly from the pulpit the sacred truth that all men are equal. He may find consolation and support in the hope of one day becoming a free man. He may purchase his freedom with money. If barbarously and unreasonably punished, he may demand his liberty and be granted it as his legal right.

He may expect liberty from the gratitude or the

190

generosity of his master, or from the dictates of a conscience-stricken master lying on his priest-attended deathbed.

And when he becomes a free man, he has a free man's rights and enjoys a real and practical equality, the like of which *merely to mention* causes, in prating and prejudiced Americans, a creeping horror and a passionate indignation!

Slavery exists elsewhere, but by force of causes now in operation, it is fast approaching its end in these countries. Let the slave trade be totally abolished (as it will be), and before half a century has passed there will not be a slave to be found in either Spanish or Portuguese America.

Alas, my countrymen, it is in the United States alone that the spirit of tyranny still soars boldly triumphant and disdains the thought of even the most distant limitation. Here alone, of all the world beside, oppression riots unchecked by fear of God or sympathy for man.

And now American slaveholders have added the last security to their despotism. In their fierce refusal to relinquish the least tittle of the whip-wielding authority, they have by special statute deprived themselves of the power to emancipate slaves. Only in Kentucky, Missouri, and Louisiana do masters retain the right to free their slaves, after meeting certain comparatively mild legal restrictions. In six Southern States emancipation is forbidden unless permission is obtained either from the county court or the state legislature—a permission obtained only with great difficulty. In Virginia and Maryland a master may free his slave providing he hustles him out of the state at once. Thus have these willful

191

tyrants most industriously and artfully closed up the last loophole through which Hope might look in upon their victims.

But, thank God, tyranny is not omnipotent! Though it crush its victims to the earth and brutify them by every possible invention, it cannot totally extinguish the spirit of manhood within them. Here it glimmers; there it secretly burns, sooner or later to burst into flames that will not be quenched and cannot be kept under!

A Note about the Adaptation

Massive architecture and furnishings, and long novels too bulky to be bound in one volume, were characteristic of the age of England's Queen Victoria (1837–1901). *The Slave; or, Memoirs of Archy Moore* was Victorian in length, close to a hundred thousand words, but in few other ways; for Richard Hildreth lacked the moral hypocrisy, middle-class stuffiness, and pompous conservatism with which many of his contemporaries viewed the world.

Hildreth's biographer, Dr. Donald E. Emerson, in noting the length of the novel, observed that it was not necessary for the hero, Archy Moore, to travel so far and wide in order for the author to present all the evils of slavery. "Hildreth could have probed the depths of the problems by searching the hearts of slave and master to find the sufferings of one and the corruption of the other. But Hildreth's strengths and purposes were different."

The intention of the adaptation is to preserve Hildreth's strengths and purposes while sharply curtailing his hero's circular wanderings. In the adaptation, one depiction of a social evil must often suffice for Hildreth's use of many illustrations of the same or similar evils.

One long section in which Archy relates his wife's experiences while they were separated has been dropped; it adds little that is new and breaks the continuity of the fugitive's story.

In the middle of the novel Hildreth introduces his chief black character, Thomas, a complex man who deserves a novel of his own. In fact, Hildreth very nearly wrote a novel-within-a-novel in suggesting the dimensions of the evils responsible for the "soul murder" of this good man. Thomas' fate had a direct bearing on plot development; this, and a suggestion of Thomas' importance as a person (to Hildreth and to his alter ego, Archy), is all that could be retained in the adaptation.

Finally, the ending of the book has been altered, for in his last chapters, Hildreth sketched the outline of still a third novel, a ten-year saga of piracy during which Archy acquired immense wealth preying on shipping off the Atlantic coast. It is here that Hildreth abandoned his passionate search for the reality of humankind under slavery.

He doubtless wrote the last chapter to preserve his own anonymity as author. By placing Archy outside the United States during the decade preceding publication of his purported memoirs, Hildreth may have hoped to insure that no one would suspect the story to be the fabrication of a "radical" young journalist who had recently returned from a long sojourn in the Deep South. He wanted the book to be accepted as the true account he felt it to be. He must also have been anxious to protect his friends on Florida plantations from the stigma of having harbored an abolitionist and from speculations about which of them had served as models for his unflattering portraits of Southern whites. The adaptation eliminates the final high jinks on the high seas and ends with Archy's escape to the North in 1836, the year Hildreth returned to Boston with his manuscript.

Hildreth set Archy's story against a backdrop of suffering black humanity and, except for Thomas and, of course, Archy, seldom developed slaves as speaking and acting characters. The few slaves brought into sharper focus by the adapter are not as much invented as they are enlarged from Hildreth's suggestive sketches. This device was used to bridge breaks in story continuity, the result of eliminating repetitious material in the original.

Paragraphs and sentences have been shortened, and the spelling modernized. At the same time, care has been taken to retain the word order and style in which Hildreth expressed himself.

Richard Hildreth

The most important issue facing the American people during Richard Hildreth's adult years (1832–65) was that of slavery. Before he was thirty, having studied slavery at first hand, Hildreth pronounced it an abominable thing and dedicated his life to doing what he could to abolish it.

His was by no means a lonely crusade. A revival of antislavery sentiment in the early 1830s had brought about an increase in the number of antislavery societies and a steady growth in their membership rolls. Slavery soon became a subject for acrimonious public debate, with the result that politicians were forced to take a stand on the issue. By midcentury a good many of them found it expedient to denounce slavery as immoral; but few who hoped to be elected were so unwise as to advocate outright abolition. Abraham Lincoln, for instance, was antislavery, not abolitionist.

Those who protested making slavery a political issue declared that "You can't legislate morals!" Hildreth

196

thought decidedly otherwise, insisting that "Politics lead to the highest kind of moral action."

Donald E. Emerson, Hildreth's biographer, tells us that Hildreth's unfriendly critics noted a "curious feverishness" in his activities, and interpreted it as an ingrained disputatiousness. Dr. Emerson adds: "It is only fair to Hildreth to observe that by no means all of the controversies in which he became involved were of his own seeking. He just expressed his opinions, and then things happened. The ensuing events rarely shook his opinions."

This gadfly on the body politic was born in Deerfield, Massachusetts, on June 28, 1807, almost two years before the birth of Abraham Lincoln. Fifty-four years later President Lincoln appointed him consul at Trieste. Hildreth's family and friends hoped that the change of scene and the mild Italian climate would benefit his health, but he was unable to hold his post for long. After resigning, he spent months of rest and travel in Italy. His condition steadily worsened, and he died in Florence on July 25, 1865, at the age of fifty-eight, and was buried in the Protestant cemetery there.

Repeated bouts of ill health were the bane of Hildreth's existence. When in low spirits he was inclined to believe that his childhood had been a too confined and studious one. Should he not have been forced out-of-doors and made to engage in the lively and boisterous sports of other boys his age, thereby building a robust constitution? Perhaps, but it might have taken some doing. The trouble was that young Richard was enthusiastically involved in the pursuit of knowledge. In the family Bible he wrote of himself: "He was the pride and delight of his Father's heart, who found him precocious, having a retentive memory, and fond of the languages and books which he was allowed to devour unmolested for years. . . ."

Richard returned his father's admiration and affection. The elder Hildreth—Hosea—was a Harvard graduate, a teacher and minister, one of the first Hildreths in a long line of New England farmers to acquire an education and enter the professions. He traced his ancestry directly to the first Richard Hildreth, who emigrated to New England in 1605 from the north of England. Hosea Hildreth was a man of considerable wit and charm, of strong convictions on many subjects including politics, and ready and eager to deliver a speech or a sermon at the mere hint of an invitation.

It happened that some of the students at Phillips Exeter Academy in Exeter, New Hampshire, wanted something other than the traditional classical education and in 1811 requested that the school offer them courses in chemistry, geology, and other physical sciences. They further requested that ethics and morals be taught objectively as "science" or philosophy, rather than strictly as theology. Hosea Hildreth was called upon to take charge of the new division, and thus, at four years of age, Richard left Massachusetts to spend his boyhood years in New Hampshire.

He entered Exeter at the age of eleven while most of the others in his class were fourteen, and one was twenty-eight. It cannot have been easy for him to be so much younger than his classmates, more precocious than most, and the son of one of the professors. He did

198

well in his studies and also became a member of the student military corps, a select group that marched out to add color to important occasions. The highest non-academic honor a student could win was membership in this resplendent company.

Richard was fifteen when he entered Harvard in 1822. Once again he found himself among students who were dissatisfied with the way their education was going. The seniors—"the uncommonly rowdy class of 1823"—instigated what was called the "Great Rebellion." Students who had traveled or had studied in Germany demanded that German methods of lecture, section, and seminar be adopted to replace the Harvard recitation room; others agitated against the efforts of authorities to maintain discipline. To add to the confusion, some of the faculty chose this time to stage a "Little Rebellion" of their own. They wanted more faculty participation in the administration of Harvard. Not much came of all this. For instance, half a century was to pass before Harvard replaced the recitation room for lecture and seminar.

Richard was to write later that a classmate of his taught one of the Harvard tutors about "equal rights" by tossing bricks through the man's windows. Dr. Emerson tells us that "Such hostility between students and faculty was the mark of proper conduct in 1823."

There is no record of what the fifteen-year-old Richard thought about his first tumultuous year at Harvard. Judging from his later statements concerning how reforms could be effected in a democratic society, one must conclude that however much he may have sympathized with the need for change, he would have deplored the heaving of bricks through windows as a way to achieve the objective sought. Before he was thirty, he wrote: "I am a party man because I believe that in general it is impossible to accomplish any great political objects, any great reforms in the administration or in the laws, except in the instrumentality of some political party." He was an active party member all his life, at first a Whig and later a Republican. But so contrary and independent was he that he often advocated a policy directly opposite to the majority party position— and not in closed caucus only but in public print, thus causing a furor inside the party and out. He believed in the political process, but "my party, right or wrong" was not part of his political creed.

After graduating from Harvard, ranking eighth in a class of fifty-three, Hildreth taught school for a year. He spent the next two years preparing for the law, was admitted to the bar, and was a practicing lawyer all his life. However, he spent far more time and expended more physical, mental, emotional, and nervous energy as a journalist and editor, and in writing political broadsides and books of social criticism and history, than he did in the practice of law.

Hildreth may well have disapproved of throwing bricks through windows as a way of changing minds on political issues, but he had no compunction about sharpening his pen and using it as a weapon in attacking what he considered to be false doctrines and the wrongheaded buffoons who advocated them. As fiery an advocate for temperance as for the abolition of slavery, he was always in the thick of political battles for governmental regulation of the sale and distribution of alcoholic beverages. When certain members of his own Whig party did not see eye-to-eye with him on proposed liquor legislation, he wrote as acidly of them as if they had been of the opposite political persuasion.

Hildreth ran for the House of Representatives in the Whig primaries in Massachusetts when he was thirty-two and lost by eight votes. The closeness of the primary vote indicates the serious split among Whigs on the temperance question. Not the opposing Democrats but the conservative Whig paper, the Boston *Courier,* let go with the following blast against Hildreth the night before the primary:

CAN ANY TRUE WHIG VOTE FOR RICHARD HILDRETH . . . notorious . . . unprincipled . . . soldier of fortune . . . ? What constitute the claimes of this *Snapping Turtle Abolitionist* . . . ? Can it be that the old consistent Whigs, who have lived and paid taxes in the city for years, and have fully contributed to support the party and its principles,—can it be that such men will lend their aid to elevate another enemy . . . ? Do they desire to elevate a thorough infidel? Do they wish to endorse the character of one who himself would be astonished to learn that he had any?

Hildreth took a back seat to no one when it came to invective and denunciation. He was a writer of violent pamphlets, published anonymously, although the name of the author was seldom long in doubt. When the governor of Massachusetts advocated a liquor bill that Hildreth disapproved of, he wrote that the hapless man was "nothing more than a mean ass, a beast of burden, owned and bitted by the rum MONOPOLY, with long ears sticking up in token of . . . stupidity and . . . servitude"; and he accused the governor of *rank* falsehood, gross inconsistency, and scandalous hypocrisy.

In answer to one of Hildreth's broadsides, the Boston *Morning Post* of January 30, 1840, had the misfortune to overstep the bounds beyond which character assassination could not go, even in those freewheeling times. An editorial sought to dispose of Richard Hildreth as follows:

"We believe that this Mr. Hildreth is insane—(members of his family have heretofore suffered with severe mental diseases)—therefore the public should judge of these violations of decency with pity for an unfortunate creature who may soon be an inmate of some lunatic asylum."

Hildreth knew the law as profoundly as he knew literature and poetry in four languages, philosophy, economics, theology, geography, and history, ancient and modern. He sued the *Post* for twenty thousand dollars. That the rash young man had the audacity to sue a mere printer for so huge a sum the newspaper announced as proof that he had at last taken leave of his senses. The matter was settled by a published apology from the *Post*.

Hildreth's profligate expenditure of energy in the political campaigns of 1839–40, coupled with his ceaseless work in abolitionist and temperance causes, resulted in a physical breakdown marked by indigestion, extreme lassitude, and spells of deep depression. Worn out, he traveled to South America to recuperate.

It was not the first time Hildreth's poor health had forced him to seek rest and a complete change of scene.

Six years before, when he was twenty-seven, he had left a beginning law practice and a burgeoning career as a journalist to vacation with friends on a plantation near Tallahassee. He remained in Florida for almost two years, where he observed and reflected upon "a different state of society and social relations" and was inspired to write *The Slave; or, Memoirs of Archy Moore* (see A Note about the Adaptation; p. 193).

His purpose, he later explained, was "to communicate the new feeling and outlook to others." Before going South he had thought slavery a bad thing; his novel was an effort to show how bad. He may have discovered the difficulty of exposing all aspects of the social evils of slavery while at the same time keeping an interesting narrative going, for during his Florida "vacation" he also wrote the greater part of *Despotism in America,* a non-fiction treatment of society under slavery. He returned to Massachusetts in April 1836, an implacable abolitionist.

His zeal for communicating his thoughts and feelings was thwarted at the outset. He found no takers when he offered to New York and Boston publishers the manuscript of what he may well have considered the great American novel. Within a few months, however, a Boston printer offered to print the two-volume novel with Hildreth footing the bill.

The author's name did not appear on the title page. This cautious approach seems justified. It had not been a year since a "broadcloth mob" had broken up a meeting of women abolitionists and had hauled the young abolitionist, William Lloyd Garrison, through the streets of Boston at the end of a rope tied around his neck. And still fresh in memory was the "Southhampton Insurrection" of 1831, led by the Virginia slave Nat Turner. In a night and a day, he and his followers had murdered sixty men, women, and children of white blood, causing a wave of shock and terror throughout the nation. Abolitionists were detested by self-proclaimed lovers of peace and order, who believed that the intemperate words of "agitators" caused uprisings among slaves who otherwise would not dream of such disorderly conduct. It was in this troubled atmosphere that Hildreth's anonymous work was launched on the literary seas, and all but sank.

Prestigious literary critics and journals of opinion ignored the work, which neatly took care of "communications" in that quarter.

The *Atlas,* a Boston newspaper, praised the author for his unusual vigor and power of style, characterized the book as an abolition pamphlet in the guise of a stirring and interesting work of fiction, but warned that some of its details were too revolting to be made public. Although the novel was obviously written by a man of singular power and strength of mind, "such books should not be published. We are aware of no purpose which they can answer, save that of sustaining and impelling a dangerous excitement." Some leading abolitionists themselves proscribed the *The Slave* because it sometimes allowed plantation owners to swear. An abolitionist bookseller in New York refused to sell it on that account. The novel sold eventually because it was laudably reviewed in Garrison's abolitionist newspaper, *The Liberator,* and was regularly promoted in its pages. Except for *Liberator* readers, few people were aware of the book.

A "respectable Boston house" brought out new editions of the novel in 1840. An enlarged edition was published in 1852 and in 1855 following the extraordinary success of Harriet Beecher Stowe's *Uncle Tom's Cabin*, and Hildreth's novel at last gained general readership at home and in England. It was translated into French, Italian, and German, and widely read in Europe.

The consensus of the time was that *Uncle Tom's Cabin* was the best antislavery novel ever written. Hildreth conceded that such might very well be the case, but he wanted it clearly understood that his had been the first. He congratulated Mrs. Stowe for having made a valuable contribution to the antislavery cause; but neither his sincere appreciation of her novel as valuable propaganda, nor his characteristic gallantry toward the ladies, could prevent his observing that Mrs. Stowe had undoubtedly read his book before writing her own and had drawn from his work some of her inspiration and example.

Some twentieth-century literary critics credit Mrs. Stowe with originality in her refutation of the myth that the patriarchal system of slavery closely approximated for slaves the security and love of family life; for her suggestion that slavery's laws were less than just; and because she discreetly but firmly touched on the painful problem of miscegenation on Southern plantations. Readers of this shortened version of the *Memoirs* may decide for themselves who *first* dealt with those aspects of the slaveholding system in a novel.

Hildreth speculated that the unprecedented popular appeal of Mrs. Stowe's novel was based on its being a religious novel and Uncle Tom a type of Christian hero. Uncle Tom was but one of a large cast of characters in Mrs. Stowe's melodrama of "life among the lowly." His was a strong fundamentalist faith which enabled him to withstand being sold away from his wife and children and at last to die almost joyfully, following a vicious beating ordered by the evil overseer, Simon Legree. Uncle Tom's death assumed the redemptive aspect of Christian martyrdom.

Mrs. Stowe's work was markedly religious and sentimental, Hildreth's markedly anticlerical and realistic. Mrs. Stowe's appeal was that of an evangelist pleading that Americans return to God and to Christian love and charity; Hildreth asked Americans to return to their senses, their humanity, and to democracy.

Among those who praised Hildreth's novel was Ralph Waldo Emerson, American essayist and poet, who said it was not only the first but the best antislavery novel. The abolitionist Wendell Phillips explained its initial failure by saying that it lacked the prepared soil on which *Uncle Tom's Cabin* had fallen, and that it had remained virtually unread for sixteen years "not because of lack of genius but because it was born out of due time." *The Slave* had been reissued during those sixteen years; and while it was ignored by the novel-reading public, it was thoroughly familiar to the activists, reformers, opinion makers, and attitude changers of the day. There is no way of knowing how much America's first antislavery novel helped in preparing the soil on which *Uncle Tom's Cabin* fell, but it cannot have been negligible.

Near the turn of the century, William Dean Howells, American author and editor, who had long been one of the books most favorable critics, said: "The impression is still so deep after a lapse of forty years since I saw the book, I have no misgiving in speaking of it as a powerful piece of realism. It treated passionately, intensely . . . of the wrongs now so remote from us [because of] the abolition of slavery, that it is useless to hope that it will ever be generally read hereafter. . . ."

When he considered the book as literature rather than as sociology, Howells recalled the impression the novel had made on him because of its "imaginative verity"— which is to say that Hildreth had created a piece of make-believe that rang true. Hildreth's belief concerning slaves ran directly counter to the received wisdom of the time, which held that black men were naturally inferior, if not indeed a hopelessly subhuman class of beings. To Hildreth, slaves were incontrovertibly human. His genius, rooted in this belief, enabled him to imagine himself deeply into experiences alien to any he himself had known; in addition, the author's insight made central to the novel a young man's search for the meaning and purpose of his existence.

That an intellectual should be an activist in political and social reform movements was particularly galling to Hildreth's enemies. Many tried to eliminate the problem by declaring his brains to be aberrant, deranged, scrambled, unsettled, and what not. One wit managed to remove them from his head (a "pointy" one?) and place

207

them elsewhere in his anatomy. The story was that Hildreth had gone to a political meeting "on purpose to cause a disturbance," and there had received a swift kick in the seat of the pants. The "remarkable youth is not like common men," his critic said, in that "the usual order of human nature is reversed . . . and therefore the exposure of his brains" to injury and the unsettling of his understanding.

Hildreth's object was to change attitudes and feelings; words, not blows or kicks, were his weapons. The *New York Tribune,* for whom Hildreth worked as principal editorial writer during the last years of his life, remarked on his disputatiousness:

> Mr. Hildreth was not born to steer skillfully between conflicting opinions. . . . His love of controversy was . . . innate and genuine; it had the force of a passion; he scented the battle afar off; he rushed into it with tingling blood and heart on fire; if he had no quarrel of his own to fight for, he was always ready to throw down his gauntlet in the quarrel of another.

In spite of a frail constitution, Hildreth had enormous industry and great staying power. What he totally lacked was patience for sham, smugness, apathy, self-deception, pretenses of all kinds, superficialities, and for whatever struck him as irrelevant to the issue under discussion: "His manners were not conciliatory. . . . He had no morbid love of gaining friends, no cowardly fear of making enemies."

Hildreth spent ten years in researching and writing a six-volume *History of the United States.* Popular acclaim once again escaped him, and once again his work caused

208

storms of intellectual and political controversy to swirl about his head. Fifty years later a critic summed up the *History* in this way: ". . . his sceptical volumes, like a cold north wind, blew away many a patriotic legend." Shortly before 1900 another critic wrote: "These volumes . . . still probably form the most valuable single work on American history."

Hildreth's biographer tells us that for decades the volumes were considered a marvel of factual accuracy and that it would have been a real consolation for Hildreth, had he lived, to have seen the respect with which the next generation of historians regarded his *History:* "He satisfied himself as best he could with the reception of his work . . . and looked hopefully to his younger countrymen for sympathizing and appreciative readers."

Hildreth had a kind of prescience about his having been misplaced in time. He signed an anonymous letter in the *Liberator* as "One of the New Generation," as if that were sufficient explanation for the unorthodox point of view expressed over the signature. He was thirty-two.

Later in life he wrote that it was useless to try to persuade people over forty to consider, much less accept, new ideas; but he had a hunch about a generation gap much, much earlier in his life. In the prologue to *The Slave* he fervently appeals to (but only faintly hopes for) readers among the "generous and heroic youth" who dare to "preach the good tidings of liberty" and to "cherish and avow the feelings of a man." He must have been disappointed but perhaps not too surprised to find there was no sizeable audience of that description at the time.

"The years with the *Tribune,*" writes Dr. Emerson,

209

"were probably the ones in which Hildreth's writing had the most influence. Certainly he had then the widest audience. . . . In the last, weary, exhausted, and embittered years of his life he found as never before an audience for his destructive criticism of the slave system."

It had taken a quarter of a century.

It would give Richard Hildreth no little satisfaction to make the scene again, a century after he left it. This version of his first-of-a-kind novel is offered in the belief that a young audience may have surfaced, in this time of revolutionary social changes so similar to those Hildreth experienced—an audience that may be more receptive to his realism, his humanism, and his passionate advocacy of democracy.

About Barbara Ritchie

When Barbara Ritchie first read Richard Hildreth's *Memoirs* she was impressed by the book's intellectual honesty, realism, and force. "It struck me," she says, "that in the character of Archy Moore, Hildreth had almost fully imagined Frederick Douglass, America's foremost black abolitionist. It is this ability to imagine himself into the minds and feelings, the very innerness of others, that gives authenticity to his fictional memoirs of a slave."

Mrs. Ritchie has done several adaptations of books for young people, including *Life and Times of Frederick Douglass* and *The Mind and Heart of Frederick Douglass: Excerpts from Speeches of the Great Negro Orator*. A native of Bemidji, Minnesota, she now lives in Denver, Colorado, and is secretary of the Colorado Authors League. She is the author of a number of picture books, and her stories have appeared in magazines for children and young adults.